BALD SPOT

Bald Spot

Stories

J. Dominic Patacsil

BROKEN TRIBE PRESS

Cover concept by J. Dominic Patacsil
Cover art by Jacob Arms

Paperback ISBN: 9781965412091

Published by Broken Tribe Press
Lawrence Landing Company
Raleigh, North Carolina 27609
United States of America
www.brokentribepress.com

Broken Tribe Press is a proud member of

Independent Book Publishers Association
 and
Community of Literary Magazines and Presses

For my Esses

CONTENTS

AN APOLOGY
TO MARLON BRANDO

I told the congressman, who was hiring a small armada of over-educated, indebted twenty-somethings to schmooze his constituents, *I'm convinced God had Indiana in mind when she created erectile dysfunction.*

He muttered something about God being a man.

It was at this exact moment that I knew I wasn't going to get the job—partially for reasons out of my control, partially not.

I think of all the radical ideas that have floated through my brain, the notion of God as woman and one with a particular penis-shrinking sense of humor is hardly the most divisive. However, at the time of the interview, my life in Indianapolis was such a stinking pile of dung that I could've argued about anything with anyone and maybe bitten their ear off for good measure.

I moderated those aggressive tendencies initially, if only because it felt strange to be upset with such an old man. Across the broad mahogany desk, Congressman Jaworski, or Jaws as he introduced himself, picked at his teeth with the edge of an envelope. He wore a brown suit made of polyester, and the few hairs that remained on his head were matted down from last night's sleep.

Jaws seemed to enjoy our shared time even less than I did. He confessed at the beginning of our conversation, before things got ugly, that the pool of applicants seemed emotionally under-qualified, the lot of us exhibiting the sort of behavior his Korean Conflict eyes deemed undisciplined and therefore unreliable.

Jaws was, to his credit, a stalwart of Indiana's 7th Congressional District. He'd spearheaded a major economic development initiative in the eighties that brought tech firms to the low-cost environment of the Crossroads of America. The move proved to be a metamorphosis for Indianapolis, transforming the city from "Nap Town" to something a little better than Milwaukee. For this, he gained a sort of political tenure, consistently winning elections among his central Indiana rivals, many of whom had worked on his staff or otherwise knew the man as a genial mentor quick to offer his hand in service.

To me, this meant diddly squat. I cared very little about this baby-looking man's political pedigree and even less about some work he'd fostered decades ago, when we were, according to my arithmetic, more than thirty years past that point.

I don't mean to come across as a new generationalist. I don't think we can innovate ourselves out of all the messes we've made of this earth. But I also don't think that grandfathering in the past achievements of old men is the only way politics should work. But hey, I'm fair enough to recognize that maybe that's just the thinking of someone like me, someone who has achieved so very little in my twenty-eight years. Sure, I have a law degree and attended undergrad with peers who have already been featured in Forbes, but the osmosis of all that hasn't sprouted the seedlings of success I saw in myself. In fact, that's why I was there, sitting at that office, yanking the pin from another verbal grenade and tossing it across the desk. I needed something, anything, to right the ship's course. So I swallowed my philosophies and sent in my piece of paper, for which I promptly received a call.

When Jaws reached out to me, I doubt he envisioned the two of us would have our horns locked in a trade of dirtying words. Yet there we were, squinting at one another, positioning ourselves for the counter-and-strike of argument.

I said, *Your limp-dick policy hasn't brought new tech to Indianapolis in a decade.*

He said, *If we could cut wages in half and not offer any of the benefits, we might be able to compete with China.*

China, China, I said to him. *How about you take a little responsibility for the fact that you're resting on your laurels while young people like myself can't find decent jobs that let us live in some fashion other than being productivity machines.*

Now that's just it, Jaw barked back at me. *You don't have the slightest appreciation for honest work. You want paternity leaves and smoothie bars in the community kitchen, but where's the elbow grease? What happened to sitting down, shutting up, and logging your time?*

I'll tell you what happened, I started to yell, *We finally took the time to think!* I was standing then, shooting an index finger into my right temple. And while that finger sent a message to turn and leave while I could, the professional ramifications of arguing with a congressman far outweighing the potential benefits of picking his logic to the bone, something kept me there, seething at his Mickey Mouse tie. If I'm honest, I have never hated anyone so much as I hated Jaws in that moment. And I'll tell you something else—it felt good.

I'm not generally the spiteful type, though this is not to say I'm immune to an emotional reaction or two. I house a Pomeranian, for example, that's inclined to shit on the rug near the sliding glass door of my apartment. And though I know it's a possibility that Bella will do her worst when I fail to let her out in a timely manner, each time it happens I'm so overcome with a parade of expletives that I end up taking an extra high blood pressure pill.

However, on the whole, I like to think of myself as even-keeled. I live by a certain credo that my parents modeled for me in their marriage: if you don't react, maybe things will change. If you don't get angry, no one will know you're hurting.

At the time of the interview, this credo had increasingly been failing me, and I couldn't help but think it had something to do with CurtDog. I hadn't seen him since the incident with Marlon Brando. It was eating me up inside, not that I would've said that.

As I looked at Congressman Jaws with sweat pooled in my underarms, I'm a bit embarrassed to admit that I wanted him to feel my pain. I wanted to transmit every woe that my young heart was feeling. I wanted him to understand.

I said, *I wonder if you can get that fat head of yours wrapped around the idea that there are more realities than your own. You may be able to shepherd the lemmings but that doesn't mean that you've ever been right.*

A normal politician would've used this moment to dial one on their corded telephone and request my forcible removable. But Jaws was such a perennial figure, an institution within the institution, that I saw him jut his lower lip out and sink deeper into rage.

I knew you were too leftist to take this position. A purple wool blazer? What are we, in Oregon? he said.

Leftist and rightist are terms made for the simple man, I said. *One who wants to draw a line in the sand and assert that there's some sort of correctness in any of this.*

There is correctness! One that's sent down from my dick-swinging god. I've been delivering that truth for forty years.

And for forty years, those few proud Hoosiers who remember they have a mind have questioned your half-lidded agenda of pigpen economics and Christian morals covered in dust.

And I guess that's just it, Jaws said. He sat up a little straighter. *That's what I wonder about all of them like you. That you applied for this job. That you submitted all your well-formatted materials and yet, you never believed in any of this. Now tell me how intellectual is that?*

I tried to hide the pain of this rhetorical stabbing, but Jaws must've seen it bleed through. He sat back and crossed one leg over the other, producing a smile as if a child with an ice cream cone.

But the knife cut deeper than he knew. It sliced through the muscles and tendons and bones, leaving in its wake an empty space that CurtDog filled like water.

I felt loss like I've never felt it right then. I became a ghost, floating out of the statehouse to the apartment I lived in, though it didn't feel mine anymore.

CurtDog could do that. He could give any space a sense of completeness. I think it had to do, in part, with his general lack of cleanliness, which meant that bits and bobs of his life, his sculptures, were always lying around: bottles of rubber cement on the bathroom floor, newspaper clippings on the couch, a collection of underwear waistbands that he'd cut and nailed into the walls. But there was something more to him, too. CurtDog lived overflowingly. He overgifted and overshared and overloved. He was a fire hydrant on a hot day in the middle of the city. He flowed at one pace, which was gushing and cool, too strong to stand in his way for any amount of time, though in the heat beyond, there was no place you'd rather be.

And I told him to grow up. It's the worst advice I've ever given. A low day in a low life that severed ties with the one gold heart I know.

He'd been working on a statuette of Marlon Brando, which he chose, for reasons beyond my understanding, to create using a small bucket of animal teeth the local veterinary clinic had offered him. For painstaking hours, he drilled those teeth, shaping them into Brando's sultry brow and his broad farm boy shoulders. The end result did bear a resemblance to the Godfather, though in a loose and imaginative way. I told CurtDog as much after a particularly frustrating day of errand running, and when his feelings got hurt, him telling me that he'd inhaled nearly a pound of tooth dust over the months he spent building the thing, my response was to belittle him. I told him, *At least you have time to play with teeth all day. Some of us don't have the luxury.*

You do have the luxury, he said. *You haven't done a damn thing since you failed the bar besides bellyache about how much more you need to study. But do you study? No. You go out with your law school friends who are making six-figure salaries now and get angry when they pick up the tab. You spend hours on your computer, claiming you're networking on LinkedIn when really I can hear the YouTube ads playing.*

His words exposed a part of my soul that doesn't see the light of day very often. The part buried deep in my chest where the Truth sits tall. She scares me. A cleopatra, a lioness, God with power as plentiful as air. I shield myself from her in self-delusion. If I don't, I worry how much more inadequate I can feel.

I grabbed the Marlon Brando in Teeth and threw it at the wall. It dented the plaster, sending the mouths of a thousand animals scattered across the living room.

In CurtDog there was only pain. His eyes gave a look of abandonment, of quiet and visible splitting. He marveled at the statue blown to bits around him as if his soul felt the very same way.

Why? he barely got out.

In that moment, I shocked myself. I doubled down on anger to disregard the regret that flooded my insides. I told him, *Don't you think it's time you grow up?*

I heard that question every day after. It was a bell that tolled on the hour. And it haunted me, especially during the interview when Jaws waved his hands to get my attention.

He said, *Lost in your brain like all the rest of them.* He shook his head disappointedly. *We need doers in this office. Not a bunch of think-tank cowboys who can quibble in esoterics until their knees turn green.*

The cord on Jaws's desk phone was thick. I entertained the idea of what it might feel like in my hands as I wrapped it around his throat. I wouldn't have strangled him to death necessarily but just enough to scare him, enough that he might taste the other side. He might've found that I, too, could be a doer. I almost fell in love with the thought.

Except, I'm not an instigator, and maybe not even a doer, and I considered that maybe Jaws was right. Was I so in my own head that I forever failed to act? Would I ever make it out?

I sat down in the green leather chair where my portfolio remained, full of all the talking points I skied right over. I pushed a strand of loose hair behind my ear. Maybe it was time for me to grow up too.

I imagined returning to my empty apartment without the job. I'd left Bella entirely too long. I could picture all the dishes stacked in the sink, the dust hanging from the ceiling fan, and a hole in the plaster made from many teeth. They were all reminders of how childish I really was. I had the thought that I'd been going about this all wrong.

Maybe Jaws was doing something honorable for the state, and all it took was a view from the inside to see it.

Why else had I gone through the exercise of the interview if I didn't at least believe in that?

I said to Jaws, *Let's level here. You're struggling to find the right person. I need a position. How can we meet in the middle?*

The words felt like immediate surrender. But what options were left? I couldn't keep doing the same thing and expect some miraculous change. I couldn't imagine going back to my apartment right then.

The pivot seemed to catch Jaws off guard. He appeared much more comfortable fighting than negotiating. When I reflected on it later, of course, this was true. But in the moment of reaction, his shock offered me an inch of territory. I aimed to exploit that weakened stance for whatever yardage I could manage.

Jaws said, *It's just not a fit.*

And I said, *Tell me how it could be.*

He shook his head. He appeared entirely resistant to the thought of seeing me, hearing my voice, altogether remembering that I existed on a day-to-day basis.

But then his grin returned. It was as if a sudden and colorful flower blossomed in his head—one that stood out in that garden of white hydrangeas. I saw the evil he possessed.

I will hire you today, he said, *if you promise me that we can argue like this twice a week.*

I said nothing initially. I just looked at him as he looked back at me with eyes that have tread on the human spirit.

Could I really see myself working for him? The thought that he would hire me just so that we could argue—I wasn't sure I had the stones to be a punching bag. Though equally, if I was sure of anything in that moment, it was the possibility that I'd never been right.

I said, *I think that could be wise for this office. Having a critical opposition at your fingertips could help round out some of the more up-in-the-air agenda items with voters.*

My thought exactly, Jaws said. He extended his hand toward mine.

I felt like if I shook it, I would become a prisoner of war. And maybe I deserved that. I looked at Jaws knowing I would be submitting myself to something no less than strife, and yet the need for punishment in me argued it was necessary.

I thought of CurtDog. I thought of seeing him on the street and telling him about my new position with Congressman Jaworski. I thought of the smooth, expressionless response he would give me because, in his world, it would mean absolutely nothing. In his world, working for Jaws was working for any suit-and-tie-wearing nincompoop with an inflated ego and a German sports car. They change their clothes and their hairdos, but it's forever the same philosophy: follow the line. Follow that goddamn line.

I imagined CurtDog asking me, *Does that make you happy?* It was impossible to stop the immediate response that, no, it didn't come anywhere close.

I wondered if I knew how to make myself happy, or if I'd spend the rest of my time chasing false idols. I wondered if I would be a bureaucratic curmudgeon in forty years who found anger in the opinions of others. How did Jaws become Jaws?

I reached my hand across the desk, and it was with a soft, satisfied look that Jaws took it in his own. He pumped my fist like he wanted me to know that he would destroy my life soon enough. I felt like wet clay. Like a seedling. Like a child. Does that make you happy? I wondered.

I said to Jaws, *I appreciate your time, but there's no fucking way I'm working for you.*

The words filled me with life.

However, Jaws did not let go of my hand. He clenched it in his own with a gaze of sudden betrayal. He yanked me forward and my legs knocked against the desk. A picture frame tipped over. It showed a woman in a grey power suit with a spine that was ramrod straight. Her cheeks were rounded with age, and in her eyes, I noted the slightest hint that, at the time of this particular picture, she likely wanted to die.

What did you say? Jaws growled. He wrenched my hand again, pulling harder this time. I fell right over the desktop, knocking over more picture frames and sending a mess of files to the floor. *Do you think this is some sort of joke?* he cried. *I've dedicated my life to this state.*

I'll tell you it's a unique position of vulnerability to be chest-down on top of the desk of your interviewer. This is especially true when the interviewer is a crotchety old man who, in the middle of a dramatic episode, seemed entirely capable of dragging me from his office to the curb, where I would develop road rash through my shirt in addition to a great gift of embarrassment.

I looked for something, anything, to stop the pulling, and found it below his belt buckle. With my free hand, I knocked Jaws in the frankfurter, and this did the trick.

He fell back onto the floor, where his brittle body crashed in a heap. Here was one of the most important men in Indiana, and he cried out that his boys were hurting something fierce. He cried out that he was too damn old for any of this. His bulbous head glowed like a stalk of rhubarb.

When I got to my feet, it wasn't fear I was feeling—but joy. Not joy in hurting an old man, but joy that I had chosen myself. In a life of pervading self-doubts, in this moment, I didn't have to be anything other than a human being running out of a state congressman's office.

I did so, but not before taking the picture of Jaws's wife and tucking it into my portfolio. I wanted the picture initially as a reminder that I would never let myself sink too deep. But when I looked at her again as I exited the office, my mind went to CurtDog.

I thought of seeing him on the street again, but this time, our interaction would go differently. This time, I wouldn't say a word. Instead, I would extend the photo and let it speak for itself. And he would take it and create a sculpture of this sad woman, crafting something that managed to encapsulate the despair I found so shattering in her—the despair long alive in me. The sculpture would be made of tampons or jelly beans or smooth stones stolen from a zen garden. And I imagined running my hands over the face of this sculpture, touching every bump and edge as if it might disappear if I didn't. And I allowed myself, in the marble hallways of the statehouse, where the footsteps of security guards marched in my direction, to imagine one moment more. I imagined the bristly cheek of CurtDog's face. Under my fingers, he'd know I'm sorry.

LITTLE BATTLES

It's the little things that remind me I'm an idiot, like, when my coworker dies and I think to text Gemma. Doyle sat at the cubicle over from me for four years, and I want to tell Gemma that a drunk driver smashed him plum into the ravine. We only just heard about it. The boss man came in with consternation and pity wrapped up in his cheeks to tell us that we'd send company flowers.

Everyone is on their phones, calling husbands and wives and mistresses and pets while I sit and look at that empty cubicle. I think Doyle probably ate more egg salad sandwiches in his shortened lifetime than I could ever achieve. I think Gemma might find that interesting.

She might pose the question as to whether or not I thought Doyle made his egg salad special or if he just bought it from the store. I'd say that if I knew anything about accountants, Doyle had run the macros. Homemade was the way to go. I try to type the words, *My egg salad coworker died*, but stop halfway.

I'm reminded of a moment just before Gemma left me. We stood in the grocery checkout line. She was reading the tabloid headings aloud and got to *Carrie Demands Divorce After Sex Scandal* before she quit it.

How do we keep going? she asked me. *When does it ever work out?* I shrugged and asked her if she thought the grocery bill would be under a hundred dollars. She said it wouldn't be and looked disappointed.

I read the text I've started and consider what can come of it. All roads to Gemma are dead. There was a time when she loved me, when we enjoyed alternative Japanese films and competed to see who could get the sweatiest ass from the spin class we both used to attend. But those pleasures ended when Gemma stepped away from me. She said she had to work on herself.

What can you do but applaud that? Saying, *I can make it better*, doesn't work. I've tried. But I want to make it better, and I want her to believe that I can, and I just don't want to be alone, like I am right now, thinking even if I sent a message to Gemma and she didn't respond, it would feel better than swallowing all of these words.

Everyone else's conversations are wrapping around my head. I've heard the phrase *drunk driver* too many times today. So many times that I find myself staring at the sticky notes taped to Doyle's monitor, wondering what he felt in the very last moment.

I have a nice thought that maybe he was at peace. Maybe he was looking into the ravine, which is green and flowery this time of year, unaware of the Ford pickup that had crossed the median. I pray this is true, and start another text message to Gemma where I fib and say it is. But something stops me from sending it.

Maybe it's that I know it isn't the truth. That it's fairly dishonorable to wax poetic when someone you know has died. Maybe it's that I know Doyle must've been screaming to high heavens or even calculating in fast math the probability that all of it was happening to him. On that road, at that time, in that spot, I put the odds at one in 6,500.

And this is my lowest. This is when I feel the idiot alive in me. I think to ask Gemma if she would take that line. I found it sexy how calculated her bets used to be—or are, I guess. Shit.

This wrecks me, the notion that there came a moment in Gemma's beautiful brain when I was no longer worth the risk.

And she can say it was to work on herself, but we both know she's shielding me from something. Something which I still can't bear to acknowledge because it will force me to forego those sweet moments, like, when we compared ass sweat in the gym mirror.

I am inadequate. I am inept. I am the cheese between your toes. How am I supposed to find my way back? I don't even know which way is up.

I have written this text at least a million times, and like the rest, I do not send it. I feel exposed by my words, by how weak I've become. Sending this will get me no closer to the feelings I try to pump with life. All roads to Gemma are dead.

I wish Doyle were here to tell me this. He had that calm and stupid way about him that could set anyone at ease.

I wonder what he's doing now. I wonder if the egg salad in heaven uses dill. I want to feel close to him.

I get up and walk a cubicle over. Nobody notices. They are distracted by their conversations, which have drifted from the original purpose to dinner plans, to picking up the kids, to the lumber sale happening at Menards.

I sit in Doyle's chair. It's a swivel back, and I do a couple of circles. I grab the desk to steady myself, but the brain inside me keeps going. It spins on and on while I study the tidy quarters of Doyle's professional life: his Casio extra large, his cup of blue and black pens, those sticky notes taped to his monitor.

There are two of them. The first one reads, *Pass: M@rth4St3waRt!*. The second one reads, *You have never been weaker. You have never been stronger. You have only been here.*

I stand and try to make it seem that Doyle's desk has remained untouched, but I'm dizzy. My brain won't stop spinning. I have the thought that I am circling the drain.

I take the second sticky note and fold it into my pocket then immediately remove it to read it again. There are three sentences. Declarative sentences. Sentences with little room for air. I read them and read them, and I start to think that these people around me, they talk awfully loud.

ARETE

I said to A, *Crazy to think some people are born in a place called Home. Must be nice.* I tried to skip a flat stone across the glassy waters of The Serpentine. It plunked without a single jump.

A watched me with her arms crossed over a grey knit jumper. A white cashmere scarf wrapped loosely around her throat. The gentle arc of her cheekbones seemed unimpressed, whether by me or my lack of rock-skipping abilities, I couldn't tell.

I said, *If I look back at my thirty-two years of life, all the places I've lived and the people I've been, I haven't known Home for some time. Don't you think that's troubling?*

To know it then lose it, A said to me. *That's the source of all pain.* In the short time I'd known her, she had a tendency to speak in this way, like a sort of modern-day Stoic. But what made A complex to me, and perhaps equally why I felt so open to her, is that she managed to balance this rooted wisdom with an enjoyment of the sort of chaos I found myself creating. A could enjoy the simple pleasure of taking mushrooms while laid out on the park green just as much as she could dissect the source of my idiosyncrasies, as she did there on the banks of The Serpentine.

I said, *I think I've done all this running because I don't understand Home.*

As in, you don't understand the concept of Home? Or is it just that you're unsure how to create it? A said.

Both, I suppose, I said. *In my head, I don't know if Home is a place, or a feeling, if it's people, or what. The most likely is that it's a combination of these things, but I just wonder how anyone really gets there.*

A nodded her head like she better understood. Her eyes were the color of blended blueberries, and they looked through me to the waters of The Serpentine, restored to its glassy state. She said, *Perhaps no one gets there.*

So I asked her, *What's the point?*

And she said, *The point is that you keep looking for a point.*

I was tempted to ask what the hell I was supposed to do then, but I felt momentarily scared by how A might respond. What if she told me that life was a meaningless string of continual decay, comprised of emotions of our own creation that can be shared but never fully? What if she said the motivating factors in my life up to that point had been fruitless and would necessarily continue to be? What if A told me that value is a perception? I felt stuck in a cyclone of my own projections. I walked over and took A by the hand.

I said, *Can I be vulnerable in front of you?*

She said, *I would prefer it if you did.*

And I said, *You scare the fuck out of me a little bit.* I lifted A's hand and brought it to my nose. Her skin smelled of rose water and coriander. She wore a long, tasteful skirt with pleats all over. The folds swayed in the light breeze of the day.

A interlaced her fingers into mine, and in this small movement, we were closer. She wore two rings, both silver, with etchings in the shape of clouds. The metal did not feel cold against my skin. I wondered if A and I could make it to love.

She said, *The truth is you scare the fuck out of me.*

My first reaction was that she was lying. I am a mid-sized white man with a college degree from a school unknown to most. My style could be considered "maximum tax return" and my looks close thereby. Being scared of me is like being scared of a pair of white socks or perhaps the yellow lines dividing the road.

A smoothed over my doubt by rubbing her thumb against my palm. She explained, *You scare me because I think you will go to extreme lengths to find what you're after.*

I didn't like that. Hadn't she just said that there was no point in searching for a point? I said to her, *Are you scared of me because I'm an idiot?*

She chuckled. *I'm scared of you because I think I might be wrong,* she said.

We were both quiet then, steeped in the brew of our admissions. A did not elaborate on what she thought she might be wrong about, and in that moment, I did not have the gall to ask.

We instead took to movement as a natural balm for the in-between space of intimacy and discomfort we found ourselves occupying then. We took the long route around the top of The Serpentine, crossing a bridge where a balding of brown ducks swam. A and I shared little more than mere observations: a dog that chased a squirrel and dragged its roller-blading owner along for the journey or a teenage couple who cried together on a green wooden bench, whether torn by heartbreak or something else, we could only speculate.

As the sky began to spit in its normal spring routine, A and I took refuge in the first-floor cafe of a posh hotel called The Berkeley. She ordered a mint tea while I opted for the flat white. The two of us shared a selection of fine-looking viennoiseries brought around on a trolley with metal wheels.

The demographic of the cafe was decidedly classical music enjoyer and/or summer home in Saint-Tropez. Although A and I met neither of those classifications, the two of us sustained by the meager funds provided by our respective graduate programs, we enjoyed bringing a certain diversity to what was otherwise a social club for those most concerned by botox appointments and champagne vintages.

The powdered sugar of a raspberry galette coated A's upper lip. She was telling me that she had been to this cafe just once before, right when she moved to London. I admittedly cared little about this previous experience, where apparently, an elderly woman had come up to her corner table and asked if she might walk her French bulldog. Her normal dog walker had come down with the flu or been hit by a bus—this detail was lost in the retelling.

I wanted to kiss the sugar from A's lips, and had she not asked me a question, I might've sprung for the temptation right then.

What was that? I asked.

A said, *I asked if you think Love and Home are connected.*

There was something quite sexy about this. About the sheer abruptness and fearlessness to get back to it. I drowned my throat in milky coffee to buy some thinking time, but coughed, and spit a bit of it into the air.

The patrons of the nearest tables all turned. One particularly sharp-dressed man slapped his newspaper down and left. I raised my hand in the softest apology I could manage and found A smiling over the lip of her tea.

You good? she asked.

Wrong pipe, I said.

A said she hadn't been able to tell.

I laughed for a moment then was brought back to center by her question. I felt unnaturally compelled to answer it.

I think because I sought both things—Love and Home—and I thought that if I found them and stuck them together, I might have one of those irresistible combinations of life. Tell me when food is worse with a little salt and pepper. Can you remember the last time you cursed Saturday and Sunday for coming around?

I said, *I think they must be connected. I've been telling myself that Home is the place where that feeling to flee it all disappears.*

And you think Love helps rid of that feeling? A said.

I do, I said. *Or at least, I think it doesn't hurt it.* She nodded and bit into the yellow flesh of a lemon tart. I could smell the citrus from across the table. The aroma made me feel hungry, starved even. In that moment, I imagined the hole in my tummy was big enough to eat all the pastries laid before us along with an entire crock of tomato bisque and a nice, crusty bread on the side.

I was thinking about doing so, my imaginary lips ringed in the red of tomato-oregano remnant, when A asked me if I felt like fleeing right then. It was a big question, and one that only seemed to gain weight the more I considered it.

Did she mean since moving to London? Did she mean with her, at that table in the street-level cafe of The Berkeley? Did she mean inside that brain of mine, which never quite seemed to find satisfaction in the world around me?

I felt the bigness of Love and Home like hot air balloons that I tried to contain with my arms. But I couldn't, and I felt myself sliding down them, falling through the sky, as those balloons kept on floating up.

This was generally how I found myself: weightless, rushing in gravity's anger toward a place more solid and ready to inflict its harm. There was no sound, save that of air curling around the wrinkles in my ears, creating a low, soft whistle. It was just me, falling, preparing for the crash the only way I know: eyes closed, teeth clenched, shoulders hunched way up toward my ears. There was a moment of calm before the inevitable pain I knew to follow, and it was in this intervening space that I felt a warm hand meet my own.

I opened my eyes. A's wicker chair was empty across from me. She knelt on the parquet floors of the cafe with my hand held in hers as if a hummingbird.

The look in her eyes was of the gentlest understanding —of warmth and security and shared emotion. A felt like my mother, and she also felt like someone I barely knew, and I had the thought that maybe the space between those two poles was pretty small.

The tears overcame me without much of a choice, though if you'd asked, I couldn't say exactly why. Only that they came, and they rushed their hot streaks down my cheeks while I held onto A for dear life.

I immediately felt embarrassed that she was on the floor when so clearly that's where I belonged. I scooted my seat back and crossed my legs in front of me, and we sat under the awning of our wooden table.

We remained like that, hands together, as the other patrons crowed to ask what was the matter. One server stopped at the table to inquire if everything was alright.

A said, *We're alive is all.*

The lingering server retreated, and after a time, we returned to our seats.

Our drinks had grown cold on the table. The viennoiseries were a fork-bitten mess. And A and I looked at one another over them, trying to understand where two people go from here.

The rain outside had dulled to a light spittle. The taxis threw puddle water onto the brick sidewalks. I looked from the streets back to A. I said, *I don't feel like fleeing at all.*

She sat back in her seat and crossed one knee over the other. She looked like this was what she wanted to hear but also that she was surprised to hear it. In truth, I was surprised to say it, and more than this, to really feel it. It's hard to capture contentedness when life generally feels like a game of catching meteorites with a butterfly net.

But there is little else to explain what I felt, watching A watch me, other than a simple peace that set my heart to a low, steady rhythm. I used to think Love was about the flutters, and in some ways it probably is, but in A, I saw it was about the steadiness too.

I lingered there and watched her grow uncomfortable, perhaps for the very first time in her life. I could tell she felt some compulsion to transact, so I said, *You don't need to say anything more than what is true.*

And so she didn't. Right then, the silence was her truth. I saw it, stingingly, for what it was: a trespass into a heart space with room for only one. And while I wanted to feel torn up about that, wanted the immediate reciprocity, I think it was good for me to linger there alone. It was hard but good to sit in that red room, where velour covered the walls and floors.

Shall we walk? A finally suggested. I nodded and folded my black pea coat over my arm.

A mash of grey clouds lingered above our heads. A and I hopscotched the sidewalk, which was pocked with grey rainwater.

In the quietness that remained between us, I felt overwhelmingly apologetic. All that peace and stillness was rifled to the wind in favor of that old reliable worry that I was going about this existence all wrong.

At the Hungarian Embassy in the chest of Belgravia, I caved in. I said I was sorry.

A was ahead of me on the sidewalk, and when she heard this, she turned in a fury back to me. It was apparent that I was not supposed to feel sorry by the angle of her eyebrows, which curved like snowdrifts toward her nose.

Why? she inquired.

I felt sorry then about feeling sorry. I shrugged and said perhaps the most honest words my brain has ever contrived. I said, *It just seems like the point when you're going to leave me.* I tapped the sole of my sneaker in a puddle.

A glanced around the street before responding. She took in the limestone that surrounded us in great Victorian structures. The street was empty aside from some children taking turns on a push scooter. She said, *And what if I did? What if I left you here and chose never to speak to you again?*

That'd suck ass, I said reflexively, and then digging for it, came up with something a little deeper. *It's like one of those instances when you show yourself and can't be accepted.*

A understood this because she had a head and a heart. Still, she pushed me. *And what if I can't accept you? Does it suddenly fade to black if you're vulnerable and I turn?*

These were, of course, rhetorical questions, and I felt somewhat belittled for feeling what I felt again.

I could shoot myself in the head, I suggested, smiling dryly. This was the nail that broke through A's seriousness. She chuckled lightly again, then seemed to feel bad for chuckling. She waved her hands at her cheeks.

We kept moving in the direction of Eaton Square Garden before A finished her thought. She said, *I hear you and see you're worried about possession, but I just wonder if any of this is meant to be possessed?* She cast her arms at a maple with a grey squirrel clinging to its trunk. *Don't you think that when life becomes all about what you have and what you don't, it becomes impossible to stay right here?*

She was sounding Buddhist, and if it hadn't spoken to me, I suppose I would've chided her reflection. But I have proven weak at existing in the now. What she was saying about possession sort of made sense.

Except, I don't understand what is left between having and not having, I said to her. *It's a wasteland I haven't explored.*

She said, *The hardest thing in life is to use your brain. I suggest, in this moment, you do.*

I wanted to feel like A was suddenly being mean to me, but I could see in the tide pools around her pupils that this was farthest from the truth. I think she saw me not knowing how to react. She said, *C'mon, I'll try to think with you.*

We sat down on a bench that overlooked a thin quad of rain-slicked grass. At the far end of the garden, a small terrier shit in the flowers, its owner surveying the situation by unrolling a small plastic bag for pick-up. Closer was a woman who laughed at her cell phone. I imagined the comedic text that must've appeared.

Use your brain, were not devastating words. These were three words I needed more than anything.

I tried to imagine the space between what was mine and what was not by closing my eyes and picturing a small sand court with a line drawn through the middle. On one side would be all my possessions, and on the other, would be everything else.

I thought that imagining all I had would be the easy part, though I felt somewhat deflated by what I turned up. My body, my family, my Nintendo Switch—these seemed to be mine at first, although, I figured I would lose each of them eventually. This body would betray me, my family would die, and inevitably, I'd break off one of the Switch joysticks in a rage. I wondered if, in this exercise, it was better to consider possessions by timeline. Items I'd have for one year or less, five years, etc.

This became too involved and I instead decided to move into thinking about those things I didn't have. My brain went immediately to the gargantuans of life. I listed off Love, Happiness, and a savings account large enough to make a downpayment on a house. And while I told myself I had none of these things, I supposed I had degrees of them, if that could count, if, in fact, they were really mine.

I got lost in the idea then that everything just sat on the line of this sand court: all the clothing, ideals, and fears. What I had today, I might lose tomorrow. And vice versa for those keeping score.

I felt proud of this deduction and also embarrassed by this deduction, as it seemed altogether simple of me. I had used my brain to really consider A's question, and the result was some one-liner you might read from Marcus Aurelius.

I opened my eyes to find A watching, not me, but the garden laid out before us. I tried to follow her eyes. Was it the cyclist at the southwest corner? Was it the spawning clump of daffodils? Was A studying the frisbee stuck way up in the tree?

Yes, I decided. And no, I decided. I had the thought that we sat at the center of the earth. It was the happy bisection of what I had and what I didn't, and as I moved, it would move right along with me.

I felt Copernican. I felt like gravity's anchor. I felt cold in a park on an early spring day next to a woman so much smarter than me.

I tapped A on the shoulder, and when she turned, I kissed her with the lightness of milk foam. I lingered close to her face. Our noses overlapped. The emotions ran loops around her eyes.

I wanted to say too much, like, *I'm home*, or, *I love you*, but at the center of the universe, there was nothing. Cars drove by us in the lowest gears possible. Their engines refused to make a sound. The cashmere of A's scarf brushed against my cheek. Her breath would've moved the wind chimes just barely.

THE EULOGY OF SLICK DICK

If you knew him, you knew him as Slick Dick, I told the mourners, who had packed the little chapel off Kirtin St. to the gills. I stood at the pulpit with my hands at the edges. The casket of my brother lay open beneath me.

Inside, Slick Dick looked like a poem of himself—dehydrated to his essential being. His formidable cheeks lacked their usual bronze color. The shrub of curly black hair that adorned his head was styled two to three degrees past manic.

Still, I looked there in the company of raw cheeks and said what I had to.

I said, *Most of us, including myself, cannot separate Slick Dick from the ideal of male beauty. Whether it was his regular inclusion in some of the most exclusive fashion shows around the world or merely the Calvin Klein underwear ad that started it all, Slick Dick was seen by eyes across this world as the possibility for grace in a man's form.*

That is what makes it hard to stand here today—what makes it hard to see this open casket. Because we are forced to acknowledge what none of us would care to: our model is here no more.

I generally believe we should celebrate the impact of a life rather than spend time in the murk of its loss. But I cannot stand here and speak to you as the brother of the deceased, the man who knew Slick Dick best, without lamenting the way he left us.

In recklessness. In loneliness. In pain. I think many of us come here today because our friend died without knowing he mattered. He mattered to me. And he mattered to you. And there's a certain selfishness pregnant in our attendance because we are haunted by the question of what we could've done to avoid this.

Today the answer is nothing. But three months ago, a year ago, perhaps that answer changes. Perhaps each of us could've shown him the love he was owed. It's terrifying to consider if we had.

I looked down at the typed words that lay ahead of me. The curve of each letter seemed inadequate.

In my pause, someone in the crowd fell and knocked their head into the back of a pew. I watched a small group of mourners sit the man up. They inspected his face. Asked what was the matter. But he shook them off. He seemed to say it was nothing.

I carried on, not quite the same. I looked down at the casket containing my brother. *But none of this is about us in the end,* I said. *We may make the death of this man our own, but Slick Dick was never ours.*

He was alive in the comfort of his own expression. We only need to look as far as the infamous Barbed Wire Suit he wore for Raf Simons to know this is true. And I suppose, whatever role you played in my brother's life, you came to find this. That his beauty encompassed more than cloth or labels. His very attention made him a creature to behold.

I can never forget the moment, when the two of us were boys living in that dreaded Bed-Stuy walk-up, that I realized my brother was important. The two of us were lying on our bellies, drawing with crayons and markers for hours. And while I was there, two years older than Slick, raving about the scaly dragons I'd created whose spouts of fire breath were big enough to burn whole cities down, my brother drew nothing but people—faces really. I asked him why he did that.

His answer was that they seemed interesting, these people he'd seen on the subway, walking home from school—wherever he'd found them. Something about them stuck around, he said, whether it was the shape of their nose or the color of their eyes or the way their belly jiggled when they laughed.

Does this not embody the human being my brother was? A man able to hone in on that one perfect detail that makes all of us—us. He was interested, and he was never disarmed from understanding that interest. Because it was from a place of love that he communicated. Always the love.

I paused then and said into the mic without really meaning to, *Who would dream my brother is dead?* I pinched the bridge of my nose in the place where a pair of glasses might've sat. The tears came all the same.

Slick Dick was still lying in the casket despite my wishes that he might jump up and run away. I bit at my lip to feel something other than the fact that my brother was dead as the ancient dead.

I think what hurts me, I said, and I imagine it hurts you too, is the thought that Slick Dick overwhelmingly loved despite existing in a dimension of pain. I didn't know his pain or at least the extent of it, and I imagine the pills were the only ones that really did.

Does that make me a bad brother? Was I in the habit of taking? I don't think it's yeses all around. I'm not saying we had a balance, or that such a thing exists, but when Slick came down with the flu ahead of Thom Browne this year, I nursed him back to health with Red Bulls and split pea soup. I answered his calls every time. I loved my brother. Every bit of me loved him, and yet there was this void I didn't know. I wonder what void exists in me that you don't know. What void exists in you. Because I've thought back to every word I can remember. All the gestures and sounds and movements. And it's not there—at least not for me. Maybe one of you knows something different.

It was at this point when a man in a pencil-cut suit stepped into the center aisle from a pew about three-quarters back. I recognized him as the one who'd smacked his face from before.

He had shoulder-length hair, which gave his head a certain bell shape that swayed as he marched toward the altar. From a distance, he resembled Keanu Reeves, though less and less the closer he got.

At the altar, he threw himself down on the kneeler positioned at Slick Dick's torso. He intoned whispery words I couldn't make out against the murmurs that rose from the chapel. There were strained and horrified looks at the man's interruption. And as the one at the lectern, it was up to me to solve it.

I'd be lying if I said I wasn't a bit miffed to leave the stand and the rhythm of my words to shoo away a mourner from the body of my brother. As I approached the kneeler and its whispering man, his eyes opened and locked onto my own. He did not so much run as stride with purpose toward a side door that led out to the street.

All of the chapel was looking there as he went. We asked the exact same questions.

Who was that? I said to the people in the front—my uncles and aunts and cousins. They shrugged at me. *No clue,* they said. *Maybe Rick Owens?* Though mostly, they just shook their heads.

I felt ready, at first, to allow the event into the annals of life's odd occurrences. I held a duty to finish that eulogy, and all but one of the mourners had stayed in their place to hear it. I owed it to them to finish my thoughts. Except, walking back up the altar steps suddenly felt impossible.

The problem was, or is, that death puts you into this headspace where you start to imagine what the deceased would've wanted. For two weeks straight after Slick Dick's death, I went out to eat at the city's best restaurants. I maxed out an Amex just to do it. Just because I knew my brother enjoyed the finest things. Because I could still do that, and he could not.

It was from this place that I found myself walking, not to the lectern as I should've, but through the side door out to the street. The eyes of the mourners felt hot against my back. But they weren't hearing the same thing I was.

They were Slick Dick's words from a birthday party some years back. He kept asking me, while we drank Portuguese wine straight from the bottle, *What's the big deal?* It was his mantra for the night and the ensuing life thereafter. *Why the fuck are we making this a big deal?*

Truth be told, I don't love this kind of thinking. To me, it's the big deals that separate events from monotony. Those are the days when dust ceases to collect on my habitual skin. They're the ruptures, the blowouts. They're a reason to break the chain.

But you've got it all wrong, Slick Dick was saying. *You're telling yourself there has to be something big going on to rock the house? Fuck that.*

So you party every day then? I asked, feeling snarky and a bit drunk.

No, he said. *But I don't feel the need to. I don't feel the need to be anything.*

Even as I stepped out into that windy fall day, I'm not sure how much I really believed him. I think a part of me felt like the interrupting man could give me purpose. A part of me never understood what a eulogy was supposed to be.

But these are not the things I heard, certainly not as I walked down Kirtin St. toward the first big avenue in a row of them. I heard Slick Dick saying that he felt no compulsion to be, and for a brief moment in my life, I could pretend to do the same.

That was honor. That was loving someone. That was remembering who they were. I clung to these false idols, as I peeked through the window fronts of every restaurant, pawn shop, and bar.

I tried to imagine the interrupting man—tried to place his pencil suit and bell-shaped head in a context where those features might belong.

I thought I had him in a bagel shop. I ran up from behind and yelled, *What the hell?* But when I got to the table, I saw the man sitting there wore an eyepatch. I'd scared half his egg sandwich to the floor.

I tailed person after person, relying on my memory, though the details of what I sought became blurry. After half an hour, I could hardly recreate anything specific. My brother, dead in a coffin, felt distant.

The last of my wits hinged on a Keanu Reeves lookalike. I trailed him at a distance for five blocks. Off 9th Avenue, the man stepped into a place called the Milk Bar. I followed him inside after counting to a hundred.

The scene that met me was all green leather and the stench of last night's cigarettes. There were a handful of patrons nursing beers in a line, but I didn't see my target among them. I asked the only bartender on duty if he'd seen a suited man, someone who'd come in just ahead of me. I said, *If it helps, he kinda looks like Keanu Reeves.*

Like from The Matrix? the bartender said, looking up from his cell phone. *Haven't seen him. You could check the bathroom.* He pointed in the general direction of away, and being that I was starting to feel more and more lost in my own head, I went there. I followed his finger.

The interrupting man was not in the bathroom. In fact, I had the whole place to myself. I stood in front of the mirror and asked questions of what I saw. The first was if I could've saved him—my brother.

I felt some surety there was blame to be shouldered, and I felt it doubly that blame was mine. I wanted people to look at me and say, *He could have done more*, because I wish I had. I wish I saved my brother.

Maybe that was impossible in his last moments, but I loved that guy. I really did. It's a silly thing to say of one's younger brother, but he made me feel like life could be worth it. I'd watch him thriving in six-thousand dollar suits, and feel like if he could make his way, so could I. We were of the same fabric. We carried so much of the same load. And now, all of a sudden, it was me.

Looking in the mirror, it all felt backward that he was the one to die. If the roles were reversed, the chapel's pews would've been hungry. An interrupted eulogy wouldn't have mattered.

What are you doing here? I wanted to scream. I turned the sink on as hot as it would go. I put my hands underneath and cowardly pulled them away. I repeated this until the skin turned red and matched the color of my cheeks.

Afterward, I took a seat at the bar. The Keanu Reeves look-alike was nowhere to be found. I considered the words I would've said to him if only I had the shot. I worked through the venom until I reached the bottom.

It was there I found nothing that changed the fact.

But in this absence, I found something else.

There was a small black frame among several in a square behind neat rows of glass-bottled cognac. It showed Slick Dick on a runway—Bottega Veneta from god knows when. He wore shoulder pads bigger than a linebacker's.

I remembered texting him after the show with admiration for how fierce he'd looked. I said something to the effect of not wanting to come across him in a dark alley. He said dark alleys had been steering clear of him for years. It was more likely we'd meet at a dive bar. And if we did, then yes, he'd kick my ass but buy me a drink after. He sent an address and said to join if I could. The whole Veneta crew was looking for trouble.

Where did you get that photo? I said to the only bartender on duty at the Milk Bar.

He staggered over and considered the square of pictures as if they'd just appeared. *Which one?* he said.

Red turtleneck and shoulder pads, I said.

He shrugged. *Must've been before me. I've never seen that cat in my life.*

And while some irrational part of me wanted to strangle the bartender for never having known Slick Dick, it was an ounce of love that surfaced. A bubble trapped under water.

I said to the bartender, *That is my brother. He means everything to me. Last week, he took his life.*

The bartender said nothing, and I didn't want him to. I just needed to say it out loud.

THE ELKO BUTTER CHASE

Lakey Sturgis took a palmful of margarine from the brown plastic tub between her feet and ran it over the cheekbones of her grandson's face. She smeared the pale-yellow spread across the boy's sloped forehead, deep into the wrinkles of his ears, working her way down the turkey skin of his throat to his bare chest, then beyond.

Just a little more, she said to Peep, who batted long, effeminate eyelashes back at her. Nuggets of the margarine stuck to them, and for a second, Lakey was reminded of nights long past when she lived in Greenpoint and Hans was still living. She looked into her grandson's globby lashes and saw her twenty-year-old self going to bed without caring to wipe away the makeup she spent so long painting on for nights of swing dancing and manhattans at Truffani's. That was before Hans's job brought them to the desert, before their daughter was born. Now Lakey was sixty-six and dying, far from any place she called home.

As she lathered the boy's ankles with the last of the margarine, Lakey told him without looking up, *Remember what we talked about. It's those first thirty seconds. If you survive 'em, you're right as rain. Two minutes will be cake, and then, Little Peep, we'll be rich.* She lifted her grandson's chin with a single greasy finger to force his gaze up to hers. His eyes, which were usually the sort of unnoticeable brown one associates with suede furniture, were piercingly clear against the yellow sheen that slicked his skull, communicating to Lakey all she needed to know—that he understood the stakes of the Elko Butter Chase and how desperately she needed him to win.

I believe in you, she said, falling back onto the five-gallon bucket she'd been using as a stool. Peep was seven, an age at which a lack of self-awareness encouraged his soft temperament. Looking at him then, Lakey knew he was, in all her estimations, bound to be crippled by a cruel world.

Ready? she said to the boy.

Ready, meemaw, he said, and then, *Should I do some more drills?* Lakey nodded without giving it much thought, which sent the boy marching into a measured routine of high knees, skips, and jumps of varying heights. Everything was very practiced, exacted with the boy's precision, though watching Peep run through his calisthenics made Lakey nervous all the same. Never mind it was some Olympic warm-up routine she'd found online. It only mattered if it worked.

She'd never been a coach before but imagined this is what it might've felt like before a big game—the bubbling nerves giving way to nausea so acidic she could taste it. Except, as Lakey watched Peep lunge into a series of single-foot skips, she recognized this was not at all what it was like. This was not a game.

Instinctively, her hand went down to the fleshy part of her tummy, as it often did those days. She probed at the lump just above her right hip, in all, the size of a walnut. Where the skin around it was soft and gave way, the center of the lump did not. It never seemed to, and that was what worried her the most. That something so small and hard could be growing inside her. That her grandson might only know loss.

###

Lakey found the tumor with a beer in hand alongside the Community Pool. She occupied a gummy chaise lounge whose fabric sagged. The Nevada sun blistered overhead.

Come get some more sunscreen, Lakey said. *I can see your shoulders are pink.*

One sec, meemaw, Little Peep replied before ramping a plastic speedboat into the air.

Over the crisp metal of the can at her lips, the day brimmed with summer glory. A June weekend with nowhere to be except beneath the great big blue. It was days like that when she missed them the most, when she wished that she wasn't alone.

Peep's boat crashed back into the water, where it bobbed over waves of his slapping arm's creation.

Peep! Lakey said, *Sunscreen now,* though when she tried to stand, she fell right back down. A swift pain coursed her stomach.

She brought her hands to a place she imagined an appendix might be and when she pressed there, she was sure it had burst. The pain dizzied her vision and caused her to slump in the chair. When she called Peep a third time, he came.

She heard his little wet feet slap against the cement as he ran to her. Lakey's eyes were closed and then open when she felt the boy's fingers going to the spot on her stomach she had covered. She must've given him a serious look then, a look that communicated severity, because Little Peep broke into a harsh sob.

You're dying, he said, and Lakey couldn't fight him. She thought she might've been.

Grab my phone and dial 911, she said. She watched him upend her handbag on the pool deck. He grabbed her big silver iPhone and pressed it to his cheek.

Help! Help! This is Peep Sturgis, and my meemaw is dying at the pool.

###

The waxy paper of the doctor's table crinkled beneath Lakey's shifting corduroy seat. Doctor Marigold perched on a miniature stool wheeling from the computer at one end of the office to the adjacent counter at the other. There, a thick manila folder was stacked high with paperwork from the last few weeks' labs and their corresponding notes. When Marigold had trekked the short distance between computer and folder three times, he removed the rimless glasses that clung to the sharp ledge of his nose and folded them into the breast pocket of his white coat.

I'm sorry, was all he said for a good long while, letting the shake of his head do the talking. *You're in for it. It's late stage*, he said after a time. Somehow, Lakey already knew.

She knew everything when she looked in the mirror of the sterile hospital bathroom just outside the oncology office. She cupped her hands under the greening faucet and tossed cold water at her face, as if all of it could be washed away and renewal lay just ahead. Most of it, though, soaked her blue linen blouse which she buttoned close around her craggy neck. The water that did make it to her face seemed futile in the end, as it was quickly replaced by tears.

She hadn't slept more than a pair of consecutive hours since the emergency room doctors confirmed it was a tumor in her belly. Peep had been there to hold her hand in the ER, and she told him he was a savior. He crossed his legs like a shy little thing and said, I'll *always save you, meemaw.*

Marigold went on to explain it was colon cancer and that the next step was a simple one. *If you wanna make it to the end of the year, we'll have to go in and cut out a bit of the intestine,* he said. The bluntness of his tone showed Lakey he was practiced in this art—the one of relating death. He was, as she thought about it, a publicist for the grim reaper's plans, and as she watched Marigold's face still wagging, his posture altogether in ruin, it hit her that she was now a part of those plans—that she might actually die.

What are my chances, she said, *without the surgery?* Marigold continued to shake his head.

You'll be gone before September. It was late June by then. The breath in her chest disappeared.

Lakey was acutely aware of the hard spot above her hip. Her right hand rested there, over that nucleus of trouble, massaging lightly as if maybe by treating the spot better than she had, it'd dissolve away as quickly as it came.

How much will the surgery cost? Lakey asked.

Do you have insurance? Marigold countered. She did—a simple Medicare policy, but only because her bridge partner, Jaqueline, coerced her into getting it. Jacqueline's own mother died penniless to treat her diabetes. She told Lakey she wouldn't let her do the same.

She produced the blue card from her trifold clutch and handed it over to Marigold. With a few clicks on the keyboard, he turned to her, *Now this is only an estimate mind you, and our finance people can probably narrow it down if you like, but if we conduct the procedure here at Northeastern Nevada Regional, you'll be due for somewhere in the ballpark of twelve to fifteen thousand, give or take your recovery post-op.*

Lakey exhaled loudly and thanked the doctor for his help. Life now had a price, and not a dollar in her pocket was hers.

Sonnova bitch, she said beating her hands against the steering wheel. She was out in the parking lot then.

She was already down ten grand on her most recent loan. Where would thousands for a procedure come from? Not from any of the banks around there, not with her credit. And the Social Security? That would hardly make a dent. Even Hans's inheritance had bled dry by then.

Fifteen thousand. Fifteen thousand. Fuck you, lump!

Lakey looked up to find the parking lot still empty. A lone road snaked the beige desert just beyond it. She knew if she followed that road, she'd plunge deep into the canyon's serrated stomach, where the pavement gave way to dirt, and eventually, if she made it that far, where two wood crosses stood next to the road.

Lakey was so alone. She wiped at her eyes preemptively, but the tears still came. Her cheeks felt raw, and as she dried them with Hans's old hanky, she caught sight of the cutout taped over her odometer. It showed Little Peep in a dark suit so big the hem of his pants wrapped around the heel of his dress shoes. The boy had his little finger pointed up at the sky.

Lakey could never forget that day, that moment, a double funeral in the sun. It was the one that confirmed her husband and daughter would never return to her. When she asked Little Peep, who was then just four, if he would offer his final goodbye, the boy stood next to both of the coffins and pointed straight up.

They went up there, he said.

Jacqueline suggested the Elko Butter Chase at bridge club the following Wednesday.

The what? Lakey said. There was such a slew of festivals, holidays, and fairs in Elko that she could hardly keep up. Just two weeks before they'd hosted the annual Hot Dog Days, a weekend-long celebration of northeast Nevada's most iconic cylindrical meat product, complete with a DIY weenie roaster workshop and complimentary Oscar Meyer frank.

You know, the Butter Chase, Jacqueline said. *Kid runs around the football field, covered in butter, and a bunch of men chase after. First person to catch the kid gets a $15,000 tax credit, certified by the state. It was part of Gómez's platform after '08 had all of us down on our asses.*

Jacqueline was what Lakey called a young grandma. She was, in fact, a grandma; it was just that her daughter had a daughter at 19 just as she did, meaning that by the time Jacqueline was 40, she'd settled into her title of Nana just as the first wrinkles of premature sun damage began to streak their way across her forehead.

Ring any bells? Jacqueline asked. She pulled thick, black-framed glasses from her face and bit at one of the arms where a line of gnawings marked the plastic.

Unfortunately, it did jog a single harrowing memory for Lakey. She'd been to the Butter Chase just once in her time in Elko, though now that she remembered it, she was shocked she'd been able to forget. The found herself recalling the scene of a scrawny young boy, perhaps eleven, rolling in a dust cloud after a particularly brutal miner caught the young lad's arm and yanked him to the dirt like a cloth doll. With a count of *One! Two! Three!* from the crowd, an air horn signaled that the miner was the winner. He threw his hands into triumphant fists over his head, and if she remembered correctly, she thought he even cried.

How does that help anything? Lakey asked. She sounded pissy without really even meaning to.

Well, if the runner makes it two minutes without being wrangled, they win the $15,000 outright, all cash. Jacqueline paused as if that was hint enough, but Lakey didn't say a thing. She traced the smooth caramel angles of the woman's jawline across from her. Jacqueline's shiny black hair was pulled straight back from her face, the same as the day Lakey met her at the Community Pool. It was a usual Saturday a year after the car crash. Jacqueline brought her granddaughter, Sierra.

I think Little Peep can be the runner, Jacqueline said firmly. Lakey nearly reached across the table to yank one of the gold hoops clean from Jacqueline's ear. The thought of Little Peep, all sixty-seven pounds of him, being wrestled to the ground by a pack of potbelly miners with hands that would never be clean—it was disgusting. A used car salesman in a polyester shirt would dogpile on top, followed by a burger chef, then a dog groomer. Where did it end?

Out of the question, Lakey said.

But what option do you have, girlfriend? You said it yourself, you can't afford the surgery. I'm talking about a free opportunity, free as air, where you could potentially pay for the damn thing, not to mention maybe just save your frickin' life.

Jacqueline reminded Lakey of her daughter when she got going like this. They would've been about the same age. Lakey looked across the table to find her friend staring bullets into her cards.

Are you gonna play? Jacqueline said. *It's your turn.* They both knew it was Lakey's turn. They knew Lakey was gonna die if she didn't have the surgery. And, most pointedly, they knew that whether it was a good idea or not, Little Peep had to run in the Elko Butter Chase.

Lakey folded her fingers over the ridge of her nose. The skin there had gone raw in the days since she learned of her predicament. She still imagined Little Peep at the bottom of a pile, his full, brown eyes beaming out at her from under the bodies with questions she would never be able to answer. She found that when she emerged from her head, her hands had tracked their way down to her stomach, where they urged the unpliable mass that composed the tumor to return to before.

Am I ready to die? Lakey asked herself. *What would come of my sweet Peep?*

She laid down her cards, and together, she and Jacqueline drove over to the city building to inquire if the year's Butter Chase runner had been chosen.

###

Mayor Gómez met Lakey and Peep at the 50-yard line of what could hardly be called a football field. The dirt plot was lined with uneven ruts from the various purposes it served: host to the Elko County farmers market, Elko County fish and game headquarters, and of course, the home field of all the local sports teams of which there were many. Dewey Field had a red chain-link fence around its circumference containing clumps of fescue grass interspersed across the open expanse at odd intervals. Lakey pointed out the latter to Little Peep, saying, *Be sure to lift your feet as you run.*

I will, meemaw, Peep said. *I will.*

At midfield, Gómez extended one of his strong, square hands to crush Lakey's own.

One of the best days for a Chase I can remember, he boomed. The mayor emitted a prevailing sense of false joviality of the order Lakey had come to associate with most politicians. She looked warily to Peep, filled then with doubt, but the boy stood strong beside her.

All it takes is two minutes, Gómez said. He squatted in his creaseless boots to look at Peep eye-to-eye. *We haven't had a runner win in all the runnings, but by the look of it, I could see you being the first.*

The margarine began to drip down Little Peep's ear lobes in the warming air. The morning was cast in a white glow, accentuating the sheen of Peep's oily skin. Lakey thought the boy's tummy looked sunken beneath the tiny piano keys of his ribs, the margarine gathered in yellow lumps at the waistband of his cotton briefs. Has he eaten enough? Is he ready? Her tumor seemed to ache as she asked the questions.

What do you think, huh? Gómez finished. *Can you handle that?*

Peep glanced from the mayor to Lakey before looking straight up into the sky. The blue expanse was aqua and nearly unblemished, save a pair of clouds just above them. The look in Peep's eyes was soft, generous even, in the face of everything becoming real. With a nod, he stuck out his fist to the mayor, who bumped the boy's buttery little knuckles with his own.

###

Three! Two! One! An air horn sounded, but nobody moved. Peep stood, legs like a point guard playing defense, as the twenty-two men circled him at the center of the dirt field.

Lakey perched at the fence, her tumor radiating a short, injectable pain beneath the red canvas blouse she wore. Her knuckles showed white as she looped her fingers through the chain link in front of her. Over her shoulder, four sets of short metal bleachers stood filled with generations of battle-born Nevadans, who whooped and whistled with the first attack.

It was a miner by the look of him. He wore a long beard trimmed into a point beneath his chin, the same color as the soot caked into the labor of his hands. He charged like a maverick in tennis shorts, closing the ten yards between the circle of attackers and Peep in no time flat.

The miner lunged low, actually getting a hand on Peep's ankle, though it slid off just as quickly, sending the man collapsing to the dust as Peep shimmied to the right with a juke. Lakey's grandson wore the brazen look of a matador, though a butter-slicked one at that.

The chase was officially on.

At the twenty-second mark, Peep had already ducked two more in a display of flamenco hips, weaseling his way from another's headlock by retracting his lubed-up neck into his shoulders like a snapping turtle. With it, and the onslaught of ten others, packed and chasing after him with all sense of strategy thrown by the wayside, Little Peep made for a gap in the bodies that would allow him to run free and clear.

Lakey couldn't help but hold the tumor with both her hands. The pain that radiated from the mass was gaining heat, pinching at her with the precision of forceps.

She nearly collapsed, propped up by the fence in front of her. That is until she saw Little Peep slide between one fella's legs, scamper quickly to his bare feet, and hustle to the near sideline while all the others trailed behind him in a stampede.

The boy was gazellian. He moved past thirty seconds, a minute fifteen, with ease. He was covered in dust by then, all but minimizing his margarine advantage, still the seconds ticked on. Peep was free. Look how far he'd made it in such an elegant fashion. How could Lakey not believe he would save her?

She'd take the big fake check that Mayor Gómez held not thirty feet away and scream into the air, *I'm getting saved! Do you get that? I'm staying here!*

Everything depended on her grandson, the gaunt powdered donut running not just for his life but hers. Lakey felt power in his lifting knees, enough power to move her hands from the quelling heat at her side. *He's gonna do it,* she thought. *Good god, he's gonna do it.* When she glanced at the short rectangular scoreboard at the far end of the field, only twenty-four seconds remained.

Little Peep stood in the far corner of what Lakey supposed was an end zone. He skittered around in short zig-zagging lines, up then back, just as she'd taught him. He listened, that boy.

But listening couldn't have prepared him, at least not all the way. The Elko Butter Chase, like so much of Lakey's life, was reduced to a great improvisation.

The band of twenty-two attackers linked arms, spreading themselves, red-rover-style, across the width of the field.

No chink in our armor, some plumber yelled, the row of them marching toward Peep. The clock ticked on: seventeen, sixteen. At fifteen, they had no choice. The wall of attackers bum-rushed, hands clasped and closing in. Lakey watched Little Peep's eyes as he searched for escape.

The tallest one, she whispered. *The only way is under.* Her gaze went down the line until it landed on an ogre, two heads taller than the others, with a button-down shirt open to the sternum. Tufts of lettuce-like chest hair poked from beneath. It was Randy Stewart, the loan officer at Wells Fargo.

Unfortunately, Lakey knew him well. He'd criticized Hans and her daughter for not having life insurance policies, for spurring her financial ruin.

You deserve to grieve, he'd told her, *not worry about money,* though his interest rates and collection policies told a different story.

Little Peep met the charging bodies with an attack of his own.

Go, Lakey said to herself. *Get that sonnova bitch.* In her mind, she was running with the boy.

She watched Peep aim right where she wanted him: at the gaping doorway created by Randy Stewart's gargantuan legs.

The attackers collapsed from the sides when they realized where Peep was headed.

Get back, get back, they yelled in unison. If Peep made it through that one man, he made it through all of them. One hundred yards of open field laid just on the other side.

The boy slid with nine seconds remaining. Lakey hadn't realized she'd been holding her breath until she gasped at the sight of Stewart, who went from his broad-based stance to stick straight in an instant, closing the gap created by his legs. Her grandson crashed awkwardly into the loan officer's shins, his head tossed back from the collision.

He tried to scramble off, crawling like a crab, but it was no use. One man was on top of him, then three more, as they held Little Peep in the dust. He kicked his feet and lashed his fists, but the three-count sounded all the same.

Lakey could not see her grandson's eyes at the bottom of the pile, but she knew them. She knew he was ruined.

The winner, a town mailman named Gotti, jumped into the air with his hands raised like a champion boxer. The other attackers swarmed him, lifting him in the air and then onto their shoulders.

Gotti needs a drink! they cried. *Get this man a drink!* The caravan flowed out to a nearby beer tent, where they were met with cheers and hollers from the crowd assembled there.

Little Peep remained on the field, lying on his back. Lakey let the congregation pass before she made her way to him. She was surprised to find that his face was not dotted with tears as she expected but staring in the softest of ways up at the sky.

He looked like a corpse. His shins were bloody with road rash from sliding in the dirt, and the rest of him was covered in a filthy concoction of margarine, soil, and sweat. This was no way for her grandson to be. The pain reemerged in her side hotter than ever.

Hun? Lakey asked. *Little Peep, my boy?* He didn't look at her, at least not right away. He seemed transfixed on the great blueness that was above them. Lakey looked there too.

She found those two lumpy clouds from before looking like wads of stuffing ripped from a teddy bear. The sky was brightening with each minute, the whole of it so crystalline she felt sorry humans ever came to explore it. She wished it had stayed pure or else she wished only she could escape into it.

I lost, Little Peep said finally. *I'm sorry, meemaw, but I lost.*

Lakey looked at her grandson, and he started crying then. The tears were blue like the sky and streaked the dust from his cheeks. Lakey got down on her knees. She grabbed her grandson's face by either of his cheeks and looked deeply there. She saw his mother and his grandfather. She saw Peep.

Lakey pushed the fringe bangs from his forehead and exposed a white section of scalp untouched by the day. The pain in her side was dizzyingly hot. She felt faint and slight of breath.

Lakey lay next to her grandson, copying his position to lie on her back and look straight up as well. There they were, the only two left on the field.

Lakey turned her head in the dust after a time and saw the boy wore a look of fondness again. His tears had stopped, though their scars still showed in the tracks left on his cheeks. Then he pointed. Little Peep pointed his finger far to their right, at a lone cloud floating toward them from the east. It was rounder and had cleaner edges than the two just above them, though altogether of the cloud family. In time, minutes or months maybe, Lakey knew the lone cloud would join the others overhead. That would make three. Right then, however, she grabbed Peep's hand. She laced her fingers in his.

VODKA WITH THE BATHROOM MIRROR

I used to think love was the breadbasket passed around at family dinner. Each hand goes in, taking then passing, and for a while that just made sense to me.

You could say that's a projection of the love that has constituted my specific life, though such platitudes are dangerous when broadly applied. If you said this to me before, back when I used to be a piece of shit, I probably would've clocked you in the mouth. And you might've stood there and spit a tooth into your palm and asked me, What the hell was that? I might shrug back at you, not because what you said was wrong or that I think I'm right, but because sometimes a piece of shit lets the fist speak first. In this particular context, I imagine the fist might say to you, Shut up, or maybe, Suck an egg, and although crude, the fist has a convincing way of conveying exactly the essence by which language fails me.

Now you might ask, What happened? Why aren't you a piece of shit anymore? And though I think the answer is written into the way I hold my spine, I say, Ana sang me a song by the ocean.

What is this pivot? you might ask. Ana. Ana. Ana. Who's Ana? I might sigh because in telling about Ana, I must tell about myself, and you will learn just how big a piece of shit I used to be.

But there is an earnest look in your eye, which is a drunk eye, a good eye, and I'm still feeling a bit guilty for imagining what the fist would've said to you if I'd let it. I launch into the story as a form of self-remonstration, and it starts with where I'm from.

Divorced parents, I say, and for a time I see you wrestle with the facts: piece of shit, love as breadbasket, Ana singing by the ocean, and now, divorced parents. Together these tidbits prove disparate but intriguing elements of my human quilt, and so I add one more to the pile.

I say, In my life, I have had three serious relationships, each of which has ended in turmoil. You nod at me to continue, and I gulp down the acid and wonder if I might stop all this talking by punching myself in the nuggets.

I'm past that, I'm reminded, though the temptation is clear. I say all the names I wish to forget and see you lap them up like a dog.

Sarah was my vegan first kiss. Kristen my real one. And Katarina, well, she put me in an armbar when we went dancing one night and caused a small fracture in my wrist.

You've not said anything consequential, you might reply, and I would nod because for some reason I see that you are now more intrigued by what I used to be even though you have the whole of me standing right in front of you.

I've not told you about Ana, I might say. She is what matters. She is the reason I'm not a piece of shit anymore.

I tell you that her intelligence is matched only by her jovial disposition. That she is strong in body, sensitive in spirit, and has this Kantian sense of reason about her. I tell you that she wears the scars of those who have damaged her in every look she gives, and yet when she smiles she promises to open herself to the world of emotions that might meet her because somewhere in her heart she believes.

Jesus, kid. You're really smitten with this chick, you might say, and I might get a little angry that you've likened Ana to a baby chicken. And then, on second thought, I might cool to this idea, seeing as Ana, in her great compassion, might actually appreciate the comparison, as it would remind her of possibility, young and yellow.

She took to me, I say. In a crowded room in a crowded bar, the sea glass in her eyes found me. And this makes no sense—not when you see Ana. Or look at me, I say, and you do. I'm a barnacle that clings to this life in hopes of not being swept away. Yet she walked toward me, placed my hand in her own, and led me to the black rocks piled on the beach.

We sat on top of them and watched the waves curl at our feet. There was far more silence than speaking. I asked her if we knew each other. She said that in some way she felt like we did. And in my curiosity, I asked exactly what that way was. She only smiled at first.

Were you horny? you might ask me. You must've been horny, and I so wish that I am a piece of shit again. What

I would do to you if I wasn't still so stuck in that moment when Ana told me we met in a song.

It's a sad song, she said. All my songs are sad.

In keeping with the ways of this world, I said. And when I looked up and saw such scars in her eyes, I wished for a second that she'd let me make her happy.

That is, of course, not how the world works—not my world at that time at least. My world then was fueled by gas station pizza and The 1975 albums. By soft drugs and hard people and the kind of volleying force that makes a man feel lost in his own head.

Without prompt, Ana sang in a whisper that barely eclipsed the noise of the waves, which crashed closer and closer to where we sat. She sang of shitty boys and feeling wasted and still showing up for love despite them. In the high notes there was loss, in the low ones remembrance, and all through the middle it was heart. A big heart, a red heart, pulsing right in hand. It was as if I'd seen too much. It was as if Ana had taken me to the secret corridors of that place in her chest and sat me down on a red velvet couch. I felt guilty that she'd let me sit there.

Maybe unworthy is more like it, you might say to me, and for once, I might agree.

When she finished her song, a great wave crashed over the rocks and soaked us up to the waist. We giggled and sat there in our soiled clothes with the moon hanging over us like a charm.

I think I saw you in there, she said. Right there at the end. Did you see me too?

I wanted to say yes, but I could not lie to Ana. I told her it was only me.

In taking my hand again, she saw what I felt: an urge to dive back and wait there on the couch, legs crossed like a loyal dog. I wanted to scream, Sing again. Please sing again.

She shook her head. It happens, she said. How brief and violent it is to strike love.

Still I drown in Ana's poetry. I drown in her wet bell bottoms walking back into the bar, leaving me alone on the rocks. I thought of jumping into the surf and letting it bash me against the shore, but I chose something different in the end.

You, in your kindness, take hold of my shoulder and though you're a piece of shit now, maybe someday you won't be. You ask what I chose, and I look you in the eyes and I tell you that I chose to walk home.

I chose to sit on my bed and dig through the museum of my heart, whose artifacts I'd stored in a shoe box. Sarah had written me a letter saying she'd quit veganism for me, and I responded by putting a chicken wing in her beer on our very next date. There was a picture of Kristen dressed head-to-toe in Aeropostale, and on it, I'd drawn a unibrow. I drew an air bubble too, floating from her mouth, and in it, there was a question. Why can't you let me in? she asked. In where? I asked, then watched as she cried mascara onto the sidewalk. From Katarina, there was a ticket stub. We'd seen Slayer in the dead of winter. She told me that she'd kill me if I didn't start acting like a man, and though I still don't know what she meant by it, I'm sure crying hysterically while fathers with chin beards punched one other was not a part of that equation. I saw all these things, these takings with no givings, with a shame that filled the cracks in my brain. I thought of my mom, and I thought of my dad, and I thought that I never had a chance. I cried my eyes out and listened to the sad music that used to give me comfort, but it didn't sound the same anymore.

You wrap your arms around me, and at first, the urge is to push. The urge is to let the fist speak, to not let you in, but that is not what Ana taught me. Ana taught me to let you drape your ugly body over mine and to feel your breath against my neck because you are searching for me. And while you might not find me now, or even tomorrow, perhaps we'll intersect and sit down on a red velvet couch, and there will be music, sweet like honey on the tongue.

ROME, FALLING

The tears rolled fat and hot from Baloney Samuelson's face as he walked into the house. It was only once he was inside, in the comforts of the kitchen with its pistachio-colored cabinets and the roaming scent of sage, that he allowed himself to scream.

The sound escaped Baloney so guttural, so felt in the heart, that Evi rushed in from the living room. She had an uncorked bottle of champagne in one hand and in the other, more concern than she knew what to do with.

Baloney, she said. *Baloney, hun.* She set her palm on the chest pocket of his windbreaker. The touch melted what little held the man together, and Baloney crashed into the collarbone of his wife. He blew snot bubbles into her blouse—the violet satin one she'd bought on vacation. Evi hushed him to calm down, to find his breath. *In and in and out*, she said.

He felt Evi work the thick glass neck of the champagne bottle up the length of his spine. He gripped her tightly, squeezing the moment's hurt into her muscled shoulders. Evi stood tall because that's who she was and what she did.

Hunny, she said after a time, *can you talk?* She wiped the last few rollers from his cheek.

He nodded and said that he could. He'd made a mess of her, leaving rings of spittle and such down her front.

Evi seemed to pay no attention to it but instead looked deeply into his face. She looked as if searching there she might locate the catalyst for such a state of collapse when usually he was more collected than taxes.

In their two years of marriage, Baloney could only remember crying in front of his wife once. It was the night of their wedding. He'd been so excited to jump in the sack with his new bride that he broke his toe on an ornamental hickory chest while attempting a running leap into the linens.

He took the uncorked bottle of champagne from Evi's hand and slugged it a good three times.

We can open another for the Willabees, he said. *They're still coming at six?*

Evi nodded. *That's the plan*, she said. *Valerie is bringing a reference letter to their doctor. Unless—*

No, no, that's fine, Baloney said. He slugged the champagne again. *I'm fine*, he said and then, *I need to sit down.*

Evi led him through the dining room, which had been set with candles and their mishmash of thrifted chinaware for the dinner party later that evening. There was palo santo smoldering in a stone dish in the living room, and Baloney fell onto the sofa just beyond it.

Is destiny bullshit? he said into the cushions.

He heard Evi sigh. She said, *There are many strong cases for determinism.*

Do you believe them? Baloney said.

Sometimes, she said. *And sometimes, I'm happy just to pick the berries.*

He turned his eyes up from the cushions. Evi sat with her hands in her lap, running a thumb over the edge of her fingernails. Even in a snot-covered blouse, she maintained that comfortable allure that had attracted Baloney all those years ago. Her brown hair was pulled back to put her eyes on full display, which were blue like a shallow cove and served to complement the single pearl that hung around her throat.

When he was weak, she made him weaker.

It was kickball, he said. *Can you believe it was kickball?* He slugged the champagne and shook his head.

What was? Evi said.

The neighbor kids are playing it. Down there at Miller's Manor.

And?

And I went for a walk because I can't figure out why the sprinkler system in the backyard won't turn on. I called Eric and nothing he was telling me worked.

We'll worry about the sprinklers later, Evi said.

But do you know how expensive that thing was? Baloney said. *The least it could do is, you know, function.*

Baloney, you're sidestepping this.

I know, he said and turned his face back into the cushions. *Promise you won't hate me when I say this?*

I promise I won't hate you if you say it to my face, Evi said. Baloney turned to find his wife's pinky extended. He locked it with his own.

I've never seen the kid before, and I'm thinking now maybe that's part of it. He was playing kickball, or attempting to, but—he was just so pathetic.

Uncoordinated doesn't begin to do it justice. And someone, presumably his mother, had hiked his jeans up to his belly button, cinched with one of those braided leather belts that was entirely too long. For chrissakes, he wore sport goggles. I mean he was a dweeb, Evi. Category A. The type of kid you point out in a yearbook and wonder how the hell they made it through all the bullying. And I know what it means for a grown man to be saying this. But I'm standing there, fuming about the sprinklers while this kid botches a routine pop fly. It's like I can see his entire life playing out in front of me. He shook his head.

Evi closed her eyes. She looked as if she were concentrating very intently on some inner mantra so as not to snap and say something plunging.

Do you think that's fair to the child? she asked.

Baloney snorted and said it wasn't. *I'm not a monster,* he said.

So why are you so worked up? Evi asked. *What's the point of this whole tizzy?*

Was this a tizzy? Baloney wondered. Was there a point to it? His awareness folded in on itself.

It took him back there, to the gravel trail circling the manor, fuming about the sprinklers. The kickball was happening to his left.

And he saw it. He saw that bright rubber ball floating against the pastel sky. He saw the boy run to meet it, his body working as if in friction with his mind, producing movement akin to the loose rear wheel on a shopping cart. The ball fell through his open hands and smacked him in the face. His sport goggles fell to the grass.

The others shouted at him to hurry, to hurry, though clearly he was blind as a bat. The boy took one step in pursuit of what must've looked like nothing more than a hazy red orb floating in green and split his sport goggles in two.

The point of this tizzy is that I'm scared, Baloney said. And though it was unfair of him to take it there, he added, *You know I'm scared for us.*

Evi knew precisely what he meant by this. Something shifted in her eyes, and she took his hand. The skin around one of her fingernails was bleeding.

And you don't think I am? she said.

I know you are, he said. *It just got me thinking is all.*

The couple had been trying for a child. They'd studied medical journals, astrological signs, online forums, and any other piece of literature (high or not), that spoke on the topic of conception. They used balms, burnt scents, and said prayers only to renounce them when nothing solid ever seemed to take.

Dinner that night was more than a social hour. The Willabees had flown to Germany for cutting-edge IVF assistance that had given them two little ones. They'd offered to make an introduction to the doctor if it made sense. To Evi and Baloney, it was the only sense that mattered. How could it be that kids were knocking each other up in high school, and these two, with only the best intentions, heard nothing from that door?

Baloney knew it was him. He'd recently taken to standing in front of the mirror to study himself for extended periods of time. He poured over every bit and bob of his composition, often exercising little more than ridicule. What did you do to ever deserve Evi? he asked himself. When did you become so mediocre?

I'm sorry for all this, Baloney said then. *Dr. Laura says putting undue stress on ourselves isn't going to help.*

Evi nodded. She looked like she wanted to say something big, something that would simultaneously alleviate Baloney and skewer him too. He imagined her saying something like, *You don't need to be sorry, hun. This is not a solo effort. But also, stop crying about some uncoordinated, kickball-playing child. It makes you seem pathetic. And if there's one turn-off greater than my distaste for men with long hair, it's for those who hemorrhage vital life because of self-inflicted feelings of inadequacy.*

Instead, all she said was, *Chrissakes, I need to stop picking my nails.* She pulled her hand from his. *I'm gonna run to get a band-aid.*

Baloney was left there on the couch with half the champagne gone, watching his wife suck blood from her finger.

###

He wandered upstairs to shower at quarter to six. The Willabees were perpetually late, one of those families who, now with a couple children of their own, regarded time in an almost Spanish fashion—a suggestion that would be taken into account against all the other forces of the cosmos.

Knowing this, Baloney sat on the tiles of the shower with the little that remained of the champagne. He used his hand to cover the mouth of the bottle. The water against the glass was almost a song.

The kickball kid hadn't left his mind. He was there, running laps through the haze of alcohol starting to thicken in Baloney's brain, which increasingly clouded out his reason.

Baloney drank more. Becoming a father was a big deal, he thought. It was a lot of responsibility to build a kid's life. He wondered if it might disappoint him.

He drank again and decided if the kickball kid were his, he would be disappointed. He figured that was not something he could say out loud.

What kind of father was that? Certainly his own hadn't been that way. Everyone remembered Old Man Samuelson with a certain awe, Baloney at the top of the list. That thin stogie chronically hanging from his mouth. The small black beret, which he'd bought in Paris as a teen and resolved to never take off.

Baloney's father had met him with a permanent respect, which served as the mainline for their mutual affection. Even when Baloney felt he didn't deserve it, such as the time he'd strung every pair of Lou Cansello's underwear up the school flag pole, Old Man Samuelson kissed his boy goodnight.

Baloney couldn't say for certain if he'd disappointed his father, though certainly in some ways he had. He figured it was better that way—remaining ignorant—and saw this as the Old Man's continued benevolence, long after the aneurysm took him from the living.

Baloney stepped out of the shower, dripping onto the bath mat. Steam clouded the mirror. He opened a hole in it to find himself, hoping change might meet him there.

He poked at his cheeks and flicked his nipples and performed a short set of squat thrusts. He was sturdy, wasn't he? Nothing about him seemed to indicate impotence, except, maybe, the flaccid way he carried his head.

Baloney rolled his neck and pulled his shoulders back. He thought he noticed a difference immediately. He saw a version of himself, which, despite his pinkened skin, was not the soft-penised debutante of a moment before. This was Baloney Samuelson, son of the Old Man who told everyone in town his boy was going places.

Baloney slapped aftershave onto his cheeks and felt the astringent burn his skin tight. He practiced the positive affirmation Dr. Laura had assigned him, though admittedly, he'd adjusted it a bit.

He said into the mirror, *You're a legend, you rat bastard. Go and take what's yours.* It was the ego stroke he needed to finish off the champagne.

Evi had laid out clothes on the bed for him: linen trousers the color of bone and a chambray shirt that begged to be torn off. Baloney slid into these feeling a wind of invigoration, feeling confidently slutty for no reason at all. He palmed an extra dollop of mousse into his hair. The champagne had his nose tingling. He would use that tingle to become a talented conversationalist. Lord knows, with the Willabees, he'd need it.

Baloney smoothed out his shirt in the mirror. In the wave of all he'd felt in the last couple of hours, it was the relief of right then that made it worth it.

Surely his own father had possessed his own doubts and inabilities, yet he nurtured Baloney absent of these distractions. I will be great too, Baloney thought. I will be great, and he wished then he could go back in time. He would travel only a few hours and he would observe the kickball kid, and it wouldn't break him to see such mediocrity. Rather, Baloney would feel inspired, and he might drop all the frustrations about the sprinkler system to teach the young boy how to catch. This was everything, Baloney thought. A divine sense of the world's workings inflated him. He saw in the mirror and his dapper self an understanding that nurturing was the thing. With his help, the kickball kid could be a star. He just about fell in love with the thought of it.

###

Baloney walked downstairs with a certain zing in his step to find David Willabee alone in the kitchen. He was an unordinary man, standing at six feet eight inches, with the majority of that height stretched over his torso, which was thin and rangy like an alley cat. In the face, David sported a blocky mustache, prematurely grey, that quite complimented the guilty look he wore at that exact moment. Baloney looked from this guilt to the man's massive hands, which mixed a cocktail over the sink.

Sarah and Jackson broke the bottle of wine Evi had been chilling, he said. *I'm sorry. I sent them out to the backyard if that's alright.*

Not a problem, Baloney said. *By the way, the sprinklers aren't working back there. Just so you know.*

David nodded as if Baloney had offered him something sacred. He shook the hell out of the cocktail mixer.

Baloney said, *I don't know what you're having but could I get one of 'em? I sure could use a drink.*

The two men stepped out onto the patio with a couple French 75s in hand to find Sarah and Jackson Willabee stuffing soil into one another's pockets. The children were scooping it by the fistful from Evi's California Lilac, strewing bits of the black stuff all over.

David yelled, *Jackson. Sarah. Here now.* Ornery as they were, the children came. Sarah was younger, perhaps three or four, and impressionable as heck. Even in the five feet they walked from the planter to where the men were standing, it was clear she got most of her cues from Jackson.

The boy pointed his sister ahead of him, as if, in getting there first, she would bear the brunt of whatever harsh words were to come. Like his father, Jackson was remarkably odd-looking. His face had taken a beak-like shape and although he was just eight years old, the boy wore a size thirteen sneaker, which looked rather clown-like against there rest of his growing form. Baloney would've been hard-pressed to describe either of the kids as cute in the traditional sense, and he was reminded of this as they stopped in front of him, their eyes downcast with guilt.

David set his drink on a low table. He squatted then, making a sort of dragon's breath sound that made both Jackson and Sarah a little squirrelly.

What did Mommy and Daddy say in the car? David said. *We need to be on our best behavior. We are guests, and Ms. Evi and Mr. Baloney were kind enough to invite us into their home. Would you like it if Mr. Baloney threw dirt all over your room?*

Yes! Sarah clapped. *Dirty room, yes!*

Jackson tapped his sister's shoulder and shook his head.

That's right, Jackson. We wouldn't like that, would we? David said. *Now what do we say to Mr. Baloney?*

Sorry, Jackson said.

Very very sorry, Sarah said. It was clear both kids were taught to be regretful.

This put Baloney in a delicate situation. On the one hand, the natural order of things told him that the kids were on the precipice of learning something, whether or not it'd stick, and that he should honor it as a semi-adult. On the other, Baloney found a certain innocent pleasure in the fact that both Jackson and Sarah had soil trailing from their pockets. His own father had encouraged him to be a great collector of things—coins, bugs, model ships, wine corks, and gemstones. If the kids wanted to collect dirt, let them collect dirt, he thought, and it was with this fondness, mixing with the alcohol that bloomed in his chest, that he told the children, *I accept your apology. I think I have something better than dirt anyways. Wait right here. I'll run and grab it.*

Baloney dashed into the garage and was back in an instant with a small cardboard box. On the side, in big black marker, someone had written, "Plastic Guys."

Baloney set the box down in front of the children. He grabbed the action figure on top: a GI Joe whose face was camouflaged with grease paint, wielding a small plastic assault rifle.

See this, Baloney said to the children. *This used to be my favorite when I was a kid. All of them did. I would make them talk and fight and go to school and play sports, and I just loved it.*

It was a relief to see Jackson and Sarah did too. Their hands went immediately into the box, retrieving Batman and the green Centurion among others.

Play with these instead of the plant, Baloney said and nodded at David that he was on his side.

Are you sure you want them playing with those? They're probably worth something at this point.

Of course. Enjoy 'em, Baloney said. He dumped the whole box of plastic guys onto the adobe patio.

David shrugged and downed the last of his drink. *We'll need another*, he said, shaking his glass.

Maybe two, Baloney said. He followed David toward the kitchen. At the door, Baloney turned to find Jackson and Sarah ogling over the figurines. *Be good, you two*, he said.

Inside, laughter filled the dining room, where Evi and Valerie had pushed the plates aside, opting to slice hunks of brie from the wedge and eat it right off the cutting board. The laughter softened when the men entered.

What's going on in here? Baloney said. *You two doing alright?* He leaned down and gave Valerie a kiss on the cheek. *Good to see you again, Valerie. Sorry I wasn't down to greet you before. My mascara—it takes forever to apply.*

Valerie took long enough to register the joke that Baloney immediately regretted it. He looked to David, as if through telepathy he might signal to his wife the flippant quality of the comment, but instead found the man staring very intently back at him to assess whether or not he'd missed the mascara before.

Evi, ever the queen, brushed this awkwardness aside by raising the bottle of wine she and Valerie had opened.

Those drinks of yours look awfully dead, she said to the men. *Baloney, why don't you grab two fresh glasses from the kitchen.*

Their eyes locked when she said this. Evi's eyes seemed to ask, *Are you alright?*

Baloney's eyes responded, *I'm feeling a little drunk.*

Evi laughed. *It's so good to see you two*, she said aloud, rubbing Valerie on the arm. *David, please, come sit with us. Valerie tells me there's been some developments on the corn-soy hybrid you've been working on?*

In the kitchen, Baloney fetched a couple wine glasses. Something gamey and caramelized wafted from the oven, harmonizing with the sage of before. Between the scent and the drinks in his gut, Baloney was dizzy. He set the glasses on the counter, sure he would drop them.

It seemed a miracle that anyone ever made it to adulthood. Being young was being subject to just about everyone but yourself. And perhaps that was what made Baloney so fond of his father—the fact that he allowed him a certain oneness. He tolerated the fads and the hobbies, the action figures among them, with a seemingly singular goal: to nurture the emotional core of this child who, through a miracle of science, carried half of his spirit.

Baloney resigned right then to be the same. He would be the coolest of cool parents, as he'd just capably displayed with Jackson and Sarah. He'd allow his children to find goodness and badness both, but to find feeling above all. Right then, Baloney sought nothing more than to father a sensitive child. The world needed more of them, he thought. And it would be his duty to protect that sensitivity when the education system and the online bullies and the blithe treatment of everyday tragedy sought to condition it away.

Baloney imagined himself nurturing this future child as a philosopher nurtures a thought: rolling it in the palms to give it warmth, to find great pleasure in the million and one routes of possibility. Even the kickball kid would be something, Baloney thought. He wanted to stamp on his own toes for thinking otherwise. It was cruel to think the boy was destined for mediocrity. It was exactly the sort of thinking he found most damaging.

With a certain hope for himself and for Evi too, Baloney picked up the wine glasses again. He was prepared to bring them into the dining room, along with twin ramekins filled with tapenade hoummos and toasted pita, except, something caught his attention from the patio.

At first glance, it seemed that Jackson and Sarah had picked up twigs and staked them into the ground as the sort of childish ritualism that comes from an active imagination. Further inspection proved that what Jackson and Sarah had buried there in the grass was not at all an odd twig but the detached limbs of his long-saved action figures. Baloney recognized the dismembered colors and plastics with a certain sickness.

What are you doing? Baloney yelled, rushing through the screen door. *Wha—wh—why did you do that?*

The children were clearly scared by his sudden emergence, by the fury loaded behind his stutters. They trained their eyes low again, pausing in the middle of a tag-team effort to wrench GI Joe's torso from his waist.

Around them was the stuff of horror. Each figurine proved a mangled version of its former self. Batman was now armless and missing his left leg too. Darth Vader had been amputated at the waist. Other pieces lay strewn about the lawn, excluding those limbs which had already found their place as posts in the ground.

But why? Baloney gasped. *What is the point?*

Why what? Jackson said without looking.

You've massacred them, Baloney said. *Every last one of them. You've torn them to shreds.*

We were playing, Sarah offered.

Clearly, Baloney said. *Playing some sadistic game of doctor. Fuck!*

The children looked at one another. Their eyes got real big. Baloney could feel it all slipping.

Jackson was the first to crack. The boy sobbed deeply as if he'd committed the worst sin his undeveloped brain could imagine. Sarah, mirroring her brother and the fright she was supposed to feel, deftly transitioned to a blubbering mess. This left Baloney angry and apologetic both. He slapped his hands against his thighs.

I'm sorry, he said to them. *I shouldn't have yelled,* but the words fell flat. He watched the two children stare into each other's eyes and cry as if one would be named the winner.

Sarah yanked the GI Joe from her brother and jammed it into the grass as hard as she could. She struck the buried head of the in-ground sprinkler and soon the patio flooded with mist.

To his right, Valerie, David, and Evi looked on from the dining room window. Baloney wondered if they'd seen the whole thing or just how it was right then:

Jackson and Sarah mewling like trapped animals while he did nothing more than look on. He offered the children no comfort. What kind of father was that? He was unfit, that much was clear. He was not at all like his Old Man.

He looked into Evi's eyes through the window and wished he could tell her that he'd be better. He would prove himself a capable, loving, and worthwhile father if it was the only thing he achieved in life.

Her eyes told of something different. Even if she'd meant to hide it, they told him that she was broken. For them, for what they'd been trying for, for a family as families are. And he saw it—at the root of that empty gaze—an understanding that maybe this was their truth.

Through the glass, Baloney thought he saw a tear. He thought he saw his wife dry it quickly with her thumb. Nothing could be certain except for the maimed form of the green Centurion at his feet. He picked it up and held it toward the window. Its head was nowhere to be found.

TENDING THE RUTABAGAS

All she did was ask me a question, and now I have something like mental illness. I can't comb the knots out of my hair or even enjoy the döner kebabs my dad brings me without hearing it, echoing in the cave where my brain's supposed to be.

K Hole said, *Who knows more about love—*

And I said, *I do.*

Let me finish, she said. *I wasn't done.* She spat in the space between us. I think this was to show that I was on increasingly thin ice, though honestly, she was difficult to read. *Who knows more about love*, she started again, glancing to see that my lips weren't open. *The human who loved once and made it last forever or the human who has loved and failed many times but keeps trying?*

I raised my hand. *May I speak?* I asked.

Go on, K Hole said. She seemed annoyed. She seemed like this whole charade of living and loving and searching for answers had stamped out any emotions she had left.

I said, *What about the third human who loved and failed and succumbed to their failure, resolving to never love again? I feel like there should really be three choices.*

K Hole undid her boots. They were brown hikers, severely ugly, which I'd suggested she order from REI. She said she liked them for the comfort, although it seemed like every time she wore them, she got a blister.

If it helps you answer the question, this third human may be included, K Hole said.

I nodded over this small victory as if I'd made some progress on the matter. *Can I take my shoes off too? I* asked.

K Hole cast her hand to the gravel between us, wet with spit. I sat down and loosened the black laces of my sneakers. I felt the breeze through the cotton of my socks. I wiggled my toes and admired their wiggling until K Hole said, *You have to answer my question now.*

I put on my thinking pose, resting my right hand beneath my chin. However, rather than think about the hypothetical, I thought about what I looked like to K Hole, who stared at me thinking. She wore the expression of a starving tiger—like she would pounce and tear me apart if I gave her even a sliver of a reason to do so. She was beautiful. I hoped then that she thought my thinking pose was beautiful. I furled my eyebrows a little extra to add some mystery.

That's a tricky one, I said. *How'd you come up with this?*

She said, *I've been thinking about leaving you.*

Of course, I'd known this to be true. We shared little chemistry outside of those odd moments of prolonged silence which filled most of our conversations.

I read once that true love happens in silence. I'd never talked to any lover less than K Hole. I took that to be a sign. I think she did too, or else, what were we doing together after eight months, cohabiting a cabin outside Rutland, with plans to sell our rutabagas at the county farmers market?

My toes started to feel cold, but I let them go on with it. I needed to think, really think. I wished I had some Ritalin.

Where would you go? I asked.

She said, *You have ten seconds to answer me before I walk.*

Wasn't she sexy? She knew just how to speak my language. She knew it'd take her more than ten seconds because she had to re-lace her boots; still, she threatened me.

I said, *Fine. Fine. You want my answer? I'll give it to you. There's a fourth person now.*

You can't keep creating new people—, she started.

You allowed me a third, I said. *There's a fourth person now. And this fourth is a very magical person— a person who is the firstborn of a supreme and all-knowing deity.*

Jesus Christ, she said.

No, but you're picking up on it, I said. *The fourth person is sent to the earth to spread mass kindness and empathy by talking a lot. They've got a well-oiled social media presence.*

You're literally describing a modern savior, K Hole said.

I think you're missing the point, I said. *You asked who knows more about love, and I'm saying it's this fourth person because god is their parent. They have the only perfect example.*

And that serves who? K Hole said. She dropped her face into her hands. She said, *I'm this close to wringing your neck.*

I said, *You can't be mad I Mr. Miyagi-ed the whole thing.*

You've given me every right, she said. Her eyes met my own. They were the closest to crying I'd ever seen them. Little red veins webbed around her dark pupils.

That's when I lost my brain. My skull bottomed out like a wet paper bag and off it went rolling. Rolling. Rolling.

It was rolling when K Hole re-laced her boots, and it was rolling when she kissed my cheek. It was rolling when she said we'd never meet again. It was rolling when I figured that was best.

Now I'm here, on my knees, digging up rutabagas by hand. The cabin is terribly quiet. I dig and I hear K Hole's last question, the one before she latched the gate. *Do you think this is the bottom?* she asked. When I find my brain, I'll know for sure.

SECOND YOUTH

The argument started over a plate of fried eggs when Magnus said fate looked down on every fat, island bastard who never learned a little self-restraint.

You're not talking about me now, are you? Barry said back, patting his gut as he would a good dog.

I am so, Magnus said. He ran a napkin over the grey thistle of his mustache, which, despite his wiping, showed the yellow glimmer of hot yolk.

The two pensioners sat in their spot, occupying the rickety corner table at Lizzie's Diner. From the adjacent window, the men could observe the hamlet's high street, Wolverton Lane, which could be hooked north to Glenbrittle, with its greengrocers and shops, or woven through a series of gnarling switchbacks to the south, where the pavement eventually ceded to the sands and a tired, grey sea at Shepherd's Chine.

Barry chewed up the last of his sausage rounds before he spoke. A smudge of grease marked his cheek. *What do you mean in saying this?* he said. *I know I've some weight to lose.*

But it's not just that now, is it? Magnus said.

Barry shrugged as if he didn't know what more it could be, so Magnus got to the point.

What are you coming to? he said, pointing then. *Packing away that nosh like it's gonna run. You think it's any wonder Sharon Payne turned you down at the open dance on Tuesday?*

She's got arthritis in the ankle, Barry said, clearly a bit hurt.

Magnus couldn't meet his friend's eyes. Instead, he watched the road, where a group of teens in matching blue nylons ran in a pack. The boys drummed away in the direction of the Chine. Their arms swung with the consistency of an old-time locomotive. For a second, Magnus was right along with them.

He was long-haired and jubilant, 60 years younger, spinning those legs of his to a league title. He was driving his knees high to charge up Leycroft Hill. He wondered if teams still did sprints out that way.

The pack of boys disappeared around the bend. Barry droned on about Sharon Payne. *Now that I'm thinking about it, she's always been a bit timid on the right, hasn't she?* he said.

Oh, come off it, Magnus said back.

Pardon?

You turned your back, and she was out for the Charleston in no time.

That's not so, Barry said.

It is so, Magnus said. *Peter Altaviste was bragging to me that he spun Sharon like a windmill.*

Barry shook his head. *What is this?* he said. *And who the hell are you to charge in here, pointing your finger at me, saying I need to learn some discipline? Last I checked, those eggs of yours lasted all of two minutes. That is, not counting that bit you've got sticking around in your mustache.*

There's sausy grease plastered to your cheek, Magnus countered. *Look at yourself.*

And when's the last time you peeked in a mirror there, Maggie? You can wear as loose a flannel as you fancy, but we can all see those tits of yours bouncing like a Sunday vicar.

Magnus cupped himself through his shirt then dropped his hands to the table.

That's low, he said.

Lower than you coming in here waging a war over my gut? Barry asked. He wiped incessantly at his cheek, but the grease mark remained.

You had no right, Magnus said, cupping himself again.

And I suppose you did, Barry said. *What, has the nephew gone and called you a wankstain again?*

I'm not gonna be telling you these things if you go spit them back in my face, Magnus said.

I'm just trying to understand it here, Maggie. You shove insults down my throat but when I dish it back, you're the one who's hurt?

I don't need this, Magnus said. *I was just trying to help.* He put a tenner on the table and walked for the door.

A fat help you've been, Barry called after him. *A very fat help indeed.*

Outside, the air was damp with fall. The grasses along Wolverton Lane were browning and half-bent from the wind blown in from the sea.

Magnus walked into the wind, away from Lizzie's and his cottage just beyond it. He'd not gained 25 yards before the holler continued behind him.

That's like you so! Running away when we can be mature about this. Barry trotted in his wake. The man's broad gut fell heavy with each step, and seeing this, Magnus felt guilty he'd said anything at all.

It's just the paper that day had announced a recent governmental initiative that would replace posties with autonomous mail delivery vehicles—the latest in a long string of initiatives intent on bringing the island "Out of the Stone Age" as it was branded. The mastermind behind it all, a bureaucrat named Phelps, claimed these vehicles were a triumph of the technological spirit, the likes of which the island had never seen. And while Magnus could hardly argue with the fella, he felt like trying. He hoped that in doing so it might soften this feeling of late—the contrition of his life lived.

He imagined shoving a finger into Phelps' chest and saying, *You've killed a fine craft in this.*

Have I? Phelps would say.

And Magnus would respond, *It removes the personal touch.*

Phelps might run a hand around his shapely goatee as if to contemplate this with genuine interest. He'd wear a look of misunderstanding common to those who struggle to see past the cold truth of numbers. Magnus imagined the metrics and optimization models that dominated the man's thinking. His brain was nothing but a big, pink mess of binary codes.

There are efficiencies to be gained, he'd tell Magnus.

Efficiencies! Magnus would shout. *When in God's name did we start to feel the need to become so goddamn efficient?*

That was the threat of losing your grip on nostalgia. It removed the emotion from choice. And in having this thought, in imagining the expletives he'd like to unleash at Phelps, Magnus wondered if that was the point. He led a life so fueled by emotion that he'd nearly lost his sense of presence. Maybe he needed to face the cold blade of discipline. He slapped his own cheeks and tried to envision what that might look like.

Jesus me, Barry panted. *What's got into you?* He stooped in front of Magnus with his hands braced on his knees.

Aren't you embarrassed, Barry? Magnus said to his friend.

Embarrassed?

Don't you think we're watching our lives become obsolete?

I don't, Barry said.

But you have to agree this meeting for breakfast every morning is a waste, right? Isn't this the last bit of freedom we've got?

Barry took a moment to collect his breath. *You grow old and you grow fat. Thems the rules, Maggie.*

Those might be your rules, Magnus said. *But look how far they've got you.*

Barry stood tall then. His form seemed to inflate, and for a moment, Magnus wondered if the man might slug him.

Instead, Barry said, *Best to be kind to those who love you.*

I'm tired of being kind, Magnus said. *I've been kind all my life. I've waited and waited and lived from the heart, and you know what? It never came.*

What didn't? Barry asked, and Magnus had the urge to spill it all—to tell his friend about every drop of emotion that had fattened him to this current state.

He turned his gaze up the road. The damp pavement of Wolverton Lane bent around the knoll in the direction of Leycroft Hill. When was the last time he'd run this bend? When was the last time he'd run at all?

Second youth, Magnus whispered.

Second what? Barry said, but there was no stopping it then.

Magnus had visions of himself in the center of that pack of boys. His nylons billowed in the wind. He could feel the measured breath leaving his mouth as he bounded forward, step by step. He imagined feeling whole and mobile and free.

Second youth! he cried out. *It's second youth, Barry!* He turned and sprinted up the road.

He closed his eyes and felt the pavement meet the soles of his derbies. His knees pumped wildly, and in the blackness of his mind, the arms on the clock stood still. He wasn't a victim of his own passivity—he never sat back and let the cosmos steer him. He saw the road and he ran it. Who could you trust but your own two feet?

In this bliss, Magnus had the thought that maybe the autonomous vehicles would do good. God knows the dogs were wild on the island. And what if all this technology really did do something? Would it be so bad to shake the dust?

He tried to concentrate on the pavement just ahead but found himself ever so distracted by a twinge of pain in his shin. The pain, he figured, was just a sign of life filling his body again. He charged round the knoll and made for the crest of Leycroft Hill.

Peering down that winding passage, where trees lined both sides of the road, he envisioned an elegant descent, where gravity would turn his legs over with the efficiency of a wheel, carrying him down to the Chine and its cold, frothy shallows.

He'd come down too hard on Barry, hadn't he? That gut stuff had really taken the piss out of him.

He turned then to see how far off his friend trailed him and found the man at least a hundred yards back. Barry was redder than a suckling hog. Sweat stained the torso of his jacket in oblong shapes. Yet he trudged on in an aching shuffle, and it was his persistence that socked Magnus another blow of self-pity.

Why did he chase? he asked himself. There was no need for that. Magnus searched for a reason given his recent behavior, though in doing so, failed to notice a pothole in the road the size of a young terrier. He stepped into it and twisted his ankle, sending him hurtling down the base of the hill into a cluster of reeds.

Pain was the first thing—blade-like pain. He looked down and was fully prepared to find that his foot had flown off in the tumble. It was with some mild relief he discovered it still there, albeit swollen as big around as a spring melon.

He allowed his face to fall into the sandy grit. That was it, he decided. Kill me now. He squeezed his eyes shut as if doing so would channel the smiting power from above to stop his beating heart. He squeezed and tried to recede into the blackness, though something lifted him from that place. When he opened his eyes, he found Barry's concern staring back at him. It was enough to produce a fleeting moment of comfort.

Are you all right? Barry wheezed. *Can we stop playing at this?* He coughed violently into his sleeve. Magnus watched his friend's chest struggle for breath as if the whole great blue above weren't enough.

I twisted my ankle, Magnus offered.

Did you now? Barry said. *I could hardly tell by the way that things puffed up in your boot.*

Magnus looked down again. *Shite*, he said. He wanted to apologize, but the pain sent him grabbing for the earth.

Barry didn't seem to notice the words caught in his friend's throat. He was too busy waving his cell phone through the air.

A lot of good this junk's doing me, he said. *No signal.*

He sat down on the ground next to Magnus, who had squeezed his eyes shut again. Barry took his friend's hand in his own and sat him up. He said, *Maggie, you're some runner.*

Magnus couldn't help but laugh and breathe and find his large lump of a friend there with him in the sands leading to the Chine. A man who, through schooldays and workdays both, had seen the highs and lows of his soul.

You're still fat, Magnus managed to say, and it was together that they tossed their heads back. Above them, the contrails of planes carved the sky, intersecting at odd intervals for as far as either could see.

THE SCRAPBOOK

Imagine a door that isn't pulled shut. Through the gap it leaves, three thumbs wide, Simon sees a sliver of the north sacristy at St. John the Apostle. The walls are brick and crowded with oak furniture full of black cassocks and white robes all belonging to the parish. Father Kevin stands in front of one of them in a ribbed white tank top. He's a small man, with a spine that bends over itself and a rim of sprouty grey hair that wraps around the back of his head. None of this strikes the seminarian watching as odd.

What's odd is the pair of brown wool slacks bunched around the priest's ankles, the blue cotton boxers along with them. What's odd are the old man's pink buttocks staring back at Simon, sheer minutes after the last of the afternoon's confessions.

The buttocks don't hold Simon at the door necessarily. It's an unremarkable backside like most. What keeps him there, spying on his teacher, is the shrill howl of a woman playing over a phone speaker.

He can almost place it. The harsh crescendos and the breathy pauses in between. It's a sound of damage or pleasure, and he can't exactly tell which, only that everything is rushed. Simon's ankles rock, his feet unsettled, but he cannot look away.

He sees the white glare of the phone screen in the priest's left hand while his right does all the work. Skin slaps like a drum. The floor seems to vibrate.

Does he see the sacristy? Does he see Father Kevin rubbing one out through a gap in a door behind the altar? Is this the love he's committed to as a seminarian?

It's the last question that does it—that causes the floor to fold. Simon falls through the void it leaves, spinning and spinning through a great black space. When he lands, the scrapbook hangs above his head—that museum of love and guilt.

###

Simon is nine. After class at St. John Bosco, he goes to Mrs. Wiedermann's with Tegan, his next-door neighbor, until Mom can pick them both up. Mrs. Wiedermann is a penguin-shaped woman with cropped grey hair like a man's. She serves cherry jello or chocolate pudding every day but only because she doesn't have a fun house. She doesn't have a dog or a Wii, only old games. She tries to get the three of them to learn backgammon on the porch. The kids have more fun trying to roll the chips into the yard.

What Mrs. Wiedermann does have are all these rooms that are off-limits. These are the only places where Simon and Tegan want to go. So they do.

When Mrs. Wiedermann falls asleep watching *Days of Our Lives* with a cold cup of mint tea in her lap, Simon and Tegan explore her bedroom. Her husband died before the kids started going there, but Mrs. Wiedermann keeps all of his stuff. Simon and Tegan find remnants of the dead man in the dresser drawers they rifle through and in boxes beneath the bed.

This stuff stinks, Simon says, holding a golf polo to his nose.

Like my Nonna, Tegan agrees. They toss everything they encounter onto the pilly carpet—crumpled bowling shirts, Bermuda shorts, hats that read the names of California beaches.

They find the magazines under a stack of white undershirts that are browned around the armpits. There are four of them, and just by the look of their glossy covers, the kids know the pages are forbidden. That makes them dive right in.

But for what? Simon says, holding up a centerfold. Tegan shrugs and says it's man stuff or something. They flip through a couple more pages before it all feels too dirty. Too grown-up. They lock pinky fingers and promise to never talk about their finding. They promise to never come looking for the magazines again. They break these promises—together and often.

###

Simon is thirteen. He's just hit for the cycle for his little league team, but his parents aren't there to see it. Dad has a client forum down in Costa Mesa, while Mom tours vineyards with her book club, The Menopausal Magistrates.

Will you be alright with Jeanie for a few days? Mom asks before they go. Simon shrugs because he's thirteen, and that's his favorite answer.

Jeanie's hatchback sits in the driveway when he gets back to the house, bat bag slung over his shoulder. Tegan is there with him. She was out riding her bike when she saw Simon headed home. She tags along because she can.

When the two of them step into the mudroom, flute song meets them. There are mental pictures traded of a bamboo instrument and Jeanie lying on her back as she plays it in some sort of calling to the skies for good sleep. She's like that. She owns a yoga studio in a strip mall, and as Simon has noted in their few days together, probably not a single bra.

He leaves his gear piled inside the door and is about to head down to the basement to watch a movie when Tegan spots a pair of leather sandals in the middle of the kitchen. They're big, clearly a man's, but much bigger than his own feet and probably Dad's too.

Tegan holds them up. She says, *What do we have here?*

Simon ponders the sandals but is distracted by the song again. It's taken on a new meaning. It's the kind of music he imagines would charm a snake. He points his finger toward it, and Tegan follows.

Of course, they have ideas of what Jeanie is doing now, and those thoughts are filthy and magnetic. They draw them to press their ears to the paneled door where Jeanie is staying. They expect to find spring squeaks or whispered instructions, but none of it comes. Instead, the flute song softens.

They try to run for the stairs, but Jeanie opens the door.

Slugger, she says. *And Tegan. What a surprise! How was the game?*

Simon turns, red-cheeked, because Jeanie knows they've gone out of their way. They're looking for something.

He finds Jeanie wearing one of his father's blue oxfords. Her legs are taut and bronzed beneath it.

Played well, Simon says. He wonders what Jeanie thinks he and Tegan are doing. He gives her a fake smile.

Behind Jeanie, a bluetooth speaker plays on the dresser. She seems to notice the two kids looking past her.

She says, *I just play this sometimes when I'm really tired. It's bansuri.*

Simon nods, conjuring ideas of why she's so tired. He knows it's connected to the sandals and the shirt. He says nothing.

When Jeanie asks if he needs anything before she goes to bed, Simon just shrugs.

Be safe, you two, Jeanie says with a wink.

It's the first time Simon considers kissing Tegan. He can tell she feels the same. They blush at one another and hardly make it through thirty minutes of Pineapple Express before Tegan says she needs to go home.

Simon is seventeen. Dad knocks on his door.

Buddy, can we talk?

Simon pulls a pillow over his mouth. The linen case grows wet as he screams, he screams, he screams.

But there is no sound until Dad knocks again. *Buddy?*

Simon hates that word. He's not his dad's buddy. He's not anything besides a body under a down comforter trying to understand how it all came crashing down.

The blinds are drawn shut. It's the middle of the day in the middle of the summer. He called in sick five minutes ago as he has too often of late. Stocking shelves at the Stop and Shop isn't going to mend the crack down the middle of his life.

Dad is a cheater. Tegan found him with Jeanie in the backseat of his Mazda at Conejo Creek Park. She was the one who called Simon.

I don't know how to say this, Tegan started, but the words eventually came spilling. Simon only listened. He wondered how long his father had used work as an excuse to crush their family.

I'm not going to lose you, Dad says then. *I won't allow it*. He sounds certain, speaks in his CPA voice, and Simon would laugh if the strength were there. It isn't. He hasn't spoken to his father in weeks. It's been a full-time job to avoid those piercing blue eyes that watched him grow, that gave him everything he has.

Go away, Simon says, pulling the pillow from his face.

Buddy, we need to get all of this on the table.

What's there to say? Simon thinks. Mom's gone. You're with Jeanie. And here I am, crushed in the middle.

Simon, Dad says when the silence lingers again. *You know there's a lot to the situation.* He crosses into his reasons why the move to Jeanie should make sense. They've been seeing each other for years. She treats him just how he likes. Simon can't hear any of it.

He doesn't care if his parents were having "troubles." Of course, he saw how avoidant they were. But none of this hits home to a seventeen-year-old boy. All he wants is for everything to go back to the way it used to be when he was sheltered from his parents' childishness.

Simon forces the pillow over his face. He wishes that in smothering himself he can condense the hurt that wracks his brain into a single swallowable pill. He wishes there was someone to hold him, or to run fingers through his hair, or at least to tell him that he'd make it out.

He sends Tegan a text. *What time you off work? Can we go for a drive?* She replies instantly.

Simon is twenty-one. He's in the Sig Chi basement pressed into the corner of two cinder block walls. Strobe lights shoot blue lines across the dancing bodies that swell around him. The tile floor is sticky and vibrates from the floor-to-ceiling speakers playing Kanye West. Red cups tip into mouths.

How many times has he been here, in this corner, observing what he's supposed to be? Faces turn up toward the ceiling and scream the same lyrics as last weekend. He's too busy watching them to realize Tegan is right there until she yanks at a button on his flannel.

Here you are, she says. *Come upstairs. I want you to meet someone from my design lab.* She's doing this too much, Simon thinks. She gets one boyfriend and the undiscussed chemistry he shares with her becomes something to offer up to others. But when Tegan turns toward the crowd and offers a hand behind her, he takes it. Her palm's sweaty. She's been smoking, he knows.

He keeps his eyes focused on Tegan's dark hair, pulled into space buns, while she weaves through the crowd for the both of them. Funny how the guys make space for her when Simon's sure they'd knock him to the floor if he tried the same tactic alone.

They climb the stairs and emerge in a big dining hall with scuffed wood floors and long tables pushed up against the walls. Tegan leads him over to a group playing Egyptian Ratscrew in a circle at one of them. Their hands slap at the chipwood after plastic-coated cards.

That's mine, bitch, some guy in a pink polo says to a girl in a painted-on green dress. She rolls her eyes, high and away, and at the farthest point from the group, they meet Simon's. He's walking up with Tegan's hand in his own.

Ceci, Tegan says. *This is Simon.*

The girl in green scooches over the lap of a brunette in pleather pants to approach them.

Tegan taps Simon on the back, his move, and he extends his hand toward Ceci. She looks at it, then at him. She has eyes the color of French roast coffee, and a nose so small he wonders if it works. Her hair flows in waves toward her shoulders, darkest at the roots and platinum at the tips. She pulls the clasp on a small gold chain toward the back of her neck. Framed then between her collarbones is a pendant of Saint Christopher—the same one Simon wears.

I'm not a grandma, Ceci says and pushes his hand away. She steps into Simon's space to throw her arms around his chest. She smells like herb smoke and expensive fruit. *It's good to meet you,* Ceci says into the buffalo check on his shirt. *Tegan's told me everything. So much. All of it good.*

Simon looks at Tegan, eyebrows raised, but she's too smug to catch it. For once, her smile doesn't give him the pang it always has.

Simon surprises himself then. He closes his eyes, forgets the noise, and hugs Ceci with everything he's got. He thinks of every hint Tegan missed, of her new boyfriend, and all of it concentrates on that hug. Right then, the woman in Simon's arms is enough. He's so taken by the feeling of giving himself up that he thinks she might be everything.

###

Simon is twenty-five. He's wrong. After four years together, Ceci isn't everything. She's an olive sundress walking in the opposite direction from his picnic table at the beer garden.

Her words still ring in his ears. *It's time.* No ultimatum. No dramatic end. It's just time. Elapsed. Complete. Beginning.

Four years from their frat party start, just as quickly as she came, she goes. Simon wants to blame the physical therapy schools that won't seem to accept her no matter how good her test scores are. He wants to blame Douglas, that nitwit at the headshop across the street from her apartment—Ceci's smoked a lot more since moving to Baker Street. He wants to blame and blame and blame. He's got all the targets in the world to aim this feeling, but he swallows them down with another mouthful of IPA. Headless Horseman, the tap list had read.

When he finishes the beer, he orders another, four more in quick succession, and for a time that works for him. The beers soothe that burn in his chest until they start to accentuate the growing sense that soon he will be bitter and alone. He's in need of company. He leans over to an adjacent table, where two women about his age chat. A boy with a plastic triceratops plays in the gravel alongside them.

May I sit a moment? Simon asks.

The women warn him with a look but don't say anything. He takes this to mean exactly what he wants and falls into the painted bench across from them. Their gossip cuts to silence.

You can keep talking, Simons slurs, but they don't. They look at him, study him with judgment, moving from his touch-pink forehead down to the tufts of chest hair that curl over the collar of his shirt.

When they don't say anything for too long, Simon says, *I work in management consulting.* He hopes this will curry him some favor, show that he's not just hopelessly drunk for nothing, that the long hours and big budgets, they can really wear on a guy. The women, though, only glance at each other, then back at him.

Do you need water or something? one of them asks. She's got small plastic gauges in her ears. A tattoo of a succulent sits on the meat of her forearm.

Probably, Simon says, and this sends her off, clearly eager to get away. Simon and the remaining friend watch her go. Then their eyes meet over a hole in the table where an umbrella stem should be. In the face, she sort of looks like Tegan.

This your son? Simon asks, pointing to the ground. The woman shakes her head without looking.

Angie's, she says.

So you're single then? Simon asks, but this seems to send her the wrong message.

The woman's cheeks go taut on the back of some sudden discomfort, as if Simon has just introduced himself as a professional puppy kicker. Everything, all of the day, coalesces right then—Ceci, the beer, this Tegan look-alike now scared.

My girlfriend just broke up with me, Simon says. *An hour ago. Two maybe.*

He hopes the truth will encourage the woman to act like the real Tegan, but instead, she only says, *I'm so sorry.*

Simon waves her off because he thinks he should. *It was time*, he says. He downs the last of his beer.

The boy digs on, using the triceratops' horns to make a hole in the gravel. Simon watches the hole grow and grow until it becomes an unbearably lonely exercise. He digs in his pocket and types a familiar name into his cell phone but turns the thing off before anything happens.

###

Simon is twenty-nine. He always feels on display wearing the seminarian collar outside the confines of the church. He senses people judging him, judging what he represents, and half the time, he isn't sure it's good.

Dad raises a glass of Cabernet to his nose and draws in deeply.

Forest floor, he says as if this should surprise. He holds the wine up to Jeanie's nose even though she's got her own glass. She nods like he clearly wants her to.

I would like to propose a toast, Dad says then, looking right at Simon. His eyes have lost their luster. In the place of that former glow is the dullness of someone who doubled down on fiscal audits to make up for emotional lack. *Three years of seminary, Si. You're gonna be one helluva priest.* He thrusts his glass to the center of the table where Jeanie meets him. Simon clinks his glass against theirs and tips the red wine into his mouth.

Mmm, he says but holds his tongue from agreeing that the wine, somehow, does taste like soil.

The server comes and places a warm hunk of baguette on each of their plates.

The menu said it's served with lamb's milk butter, Jeanie tells Dad. He smiles and says it's fitting. He looks at Simon.

Around them are the ritzy of Menlo Park and Atherton. Tech bros in sculpted blazers sit alongside divorcees with Lexapro in their eyes. Children with iPads compete with the pianist by the bar to make the loudest noise. Simon surveys the scene until he finds a familiar face watching from across the restaurant. It smiles, and he does too. How long had it been?

Tegan, he says, walking up to the table. He nods at the man across from her, who has floppy bleached hair and a black mustache. Simon learns his name is Griff.

He's a DJ, Tegan says, and when her eyes meet Simon's, he sees she's already over it. He sees Griff is another dead end of the dating game, and he doesn't even have a clue. Instead, he tells Simon about the gigs he's playing this coming month.

I'm bumping at Origin, The Grand, you name it, Griff says.

Simon nods with a nascent knowledge of the warehouses by the wharf. He points to the seminarian collar around his throat. *Don't do too much clubbing anymore*, he says.

Tegan laughs. Simon hears their history in it.

Griff says, *Well, pull up, man. If you let me know beforehand, we'll get you bottle service.* Simon chuckles but the look Griff gives him shows he's serious.

Is that your dad you're here with? Tegan asks.

Simon turns to his table. *Yep. Him and Jeanie wanted to take me out to celebrate the end of my third year of seminary.* He clicks his tongue. *I'm still very much a boy.*

Tegan laughs again but lighter than before. She grabs Simon's wrist. *That must be weird,* she says. *Still, after all these years.*

Simon looks from Griff, who's scrolling on his phone, back to her. He could always be honest with Tegan, and he's reminded that it doesn't stop now, even if he hasn't seen her in years.

It is, he says with a nod. He can't help but feel like a teenager again in admitting this. *But not weirder than not seeing you in, like, forever. What the heck, Tee? How are you?*

Tired mostly, she says. *The Bay is killing me.* She talks work, family—the spiel. *I'm sorry about Ceci,* she says when she's finished. She sucks her teeth after saying this.

Simon nods. Says it's water under the bridge like he's supposed to. He adds, *She was jealous of us, you know. When we left SC, she didn't want me talking to you.*

Tegan shrugs. In her soft cheeks, Simon can see she knows this already. He nearly melts.

He wants to apologize, and he can see she does too, but neither of them speaks. A silence steps in between them, and they're just looking at one another to see if there is peace.

Yo, check this, Griff says, and he shoves his phone into the middle of the table to show a video of lasers and sparklers shooting from a stage where the DJ drips with sweat. *This was Carl Cox's set in Ibiza last night*, Griff says. *Guy's ridiculoso good.*

Simon takes this as his cue. He shakes Griff's hand and says it's been a pleasure. Tegan stands to give him a hug.

It's so good to see you, she says. *Let's not let it be another few years.* When she embraces Simon, he meets her without question. She feels frail, but he doesn't say this.

He says so only she can hear, *I'll call you sometime. I've got the same phone number.*

The scrapbook closes, and Simon wakes to knocking. Father Kevin is on his knees above him, rapping his knuckles on the wood floor beside his head.

Simon. Simon, buddy? Are you alright? he says.

Simon blinks three times, the blurred lines fading with each, until all that remains are Father Kevin's black-rimmed glasses and the concern of the man behind them.

Oh, thank heavens, Father Kevin says, but when he extends his hand to touch Simon's forehead, the seminarian recoils. It freezes the hand midair. Father Kevin's grey eyes ask for a reason. He reaches again like Simon has made a mistake.

You're concussed, he says, but Simon is lucid enough to slap the priest's fingers away. Father Kevin brings his rejected hand to his heart. The slow realization treads across his face.

You saw then, he says. It's not a question. The priest retreats to a chair along the rear wall.

Simon finds it hard to come by the words. The scrapbook has shown him everything.

Does he start from the beginning with the porn at Mrs. Wiedermann's? How he searched the internet for more that night? If he does, he must say that he found it in abundance. He told Tegan, and she told him how she'd done the same.

This is part of what made Jeanie impassable that night with her tan legs under Dad's shirt. *Be safe, you two,* she said. It was the first time the sexual possibilities of Simon and Tegan had been spoken into existence. It introduced the idea that the two of them, together, could be unsafe.

Father Kevin asks, *Simon, you did see me then?*

He saw more than he'd like to admit. He saw himself at seventeen screaming into a pillow while Dad knocked endlessly at the door. He saw himself riding shotgun in Tegan's Honda—the way her hair flowed over the headrest with the windows down. It was escape he sought but also comfort. And with little of either, Simon saw himself start to send those tangled wishes through the ceiling as if in doing so, he might be saved. He asked big questions that flew impossibly up, soaring like great pop flies. He imagined them landing on a desk where the two largest hands that have ever existed would catch it all and reply.

It took a while for the responses to float back. The time he hugged Ceci in the Sig Chi dining hall may've been one of the first. He felt so consumed by her sudden intrigue, by Tegan's intent to sell him off, that he did not think. He trusted their matching necklaces, and in it, a faith was formed.

It was faith he leaned on when the long exposure to Ceci's faults made him doubt the love built between them. Simon relied on the answers from the sky to manage what he noticed: the way she only wanted to have sex after she'd been out with her friends. The way she prompted him for compliments. The way she cut him off from Tegan.

Simon told all this to the ceiling, and the ceiling replied, *Soon you'll get your answer*. He listened, and all the depth he'd built with Ceci shallowed in a matter of months. She called it at the beer garden. *It's time*, she said.

It's time, Simon heard, saying it back to himself. He drank like he knew what it meant.

Could he go to Tegan knowing the last time they'd spoken he'd been short and also a bit cruel? What did he expect to find? That she'd been waiting for him? That she loved him back? Like the boy with the triceratops, he saw the hole deepening before him. He had to choose something that wouldn't hurt him.

Simon entered the seminary with the belief that his skyward conversations were the balm. He committed himself to those words. He tried to give all his love to faith, give it all to the Church, but there would always be a hole in him.

It was something he assumed could be tided over with friendship or plugged with work ethic. It wasn't until he saw Tegan with the DJ six months ago that he started to believe in the way he wanted most.

As he walked back to his table to sit with Dad and Jeanie, he recognized that hole would never leave him. There was a place in his heart reserved for red love. The kind that called into question his commitments. The kind that asked what you know and what you don't.

I saw you, Simon says to Father Kevin. He stands, and the priest doesn't stop him.

Outside, the bell tower tolls in deep, soulful rings. Simon removes the collar from his throat. He sets it to the wind, where it twirls over itself like an oak leaf in autumn. He sends a text as he marches down Boswell. *What time you off work?* he asks. *Go for a drive?* There is a buzz in his pocket almost instantly.

MAKING A MUSIC GUY

I met the singer on one of the many walks I find myself taking these days.

Excuse me, he said. *Excuse me, sir, but you seem like a music guy.* It was this last bit that stopped me from marching right along, nodding behind my dark sunglasses as if I had somewhere to be. I'm a painter, or more precisely, I used to be a painter back when life seemed more precedented. Now, I suppose you'd call me a basement dweller, a cycling sub sandwich deliveryman, or even a schlepper with an unhealthy level of skepticism that I'll ever recover my wits. So yes, excuse me if I indulged in the circumstance of the singer and fancied myself a music guy, but really, what did it matter this once?

That's me, I said, pulling my shoulders back as if he'd never made a more correct assessment.

The singer had a beard, and he thrashed at it with both of his hands before he made his pitch. *I sing*, he said, *I mean—I'd like to sing for you, and if you like it, you know, genuinely, maybe you'd have something to give me.*

My hand went immediately to the pocket of my sweatpants where two ten-dollar bills were folded.

I don't want your pity or nothing, the singer said. *I just need to get back home.*

I observed the singer closer then. His skin was burnt several hues past comfort. Smudges of dirt wrapped around his ankle bones. The mesh on his tennis shoes had worn through at the toes.

Where's home? I asked.

He said, *Do you want me to sing or not?*

I said, *I do, I do*, then remembering my role, added, *I'm a music guy. I know people in the industry.*

The singer gave me a grave look. He took a gulp and let it rip.

I hadn't expected Sinatra, though, to be fair, I don't know if I expected the singer to actually, you know, sing. It seemed just as likely that he would do the chicken dance or clop me upside the head for so flagrantly lying to his face. But sing he did, unleashing a fortuitous baritone that reverberated like a great big drum. The sonorous wave rose and rose before falling in a great anguish, the whole of it threaded with a certain pain I sniffed as real and truly felt. The singer held the last note, a low one, for a good long while until it slowly melded into his breath.

His eyes rose from the sidewalk as he asked that difficult question: what was his heart worth to me? *Genuinely*, he said, *I don't want your sympathy, alright? But what did you think?*

Great. Wonderful. Marvelous. Language seemed too coarse in that moment to capture the flutter in my chest. The singer had lodged a kernel of felt-sense in me, and I continued to hear it, that deep earnestness in his voice, as if he'd not sung but labored over something excruciatingly hot and troublesome. I felt for the bills in my pocket again.

You were great, I said, *Honest to god*. The singer nodded, clearly appreciative but craving more. He'd opened himself up and shown me the way a heart can split. And I was meant to transact for this. It pains me now to think I didn't.

I patted my pockets flat. *It's just that my wallet—I left it back at the house.* I pointed as if it mattered to the singer, but he only closed his eyes. When he opened them, a single tear rolled down his cheek, but he quickly wiped it away.

I was still hearing him mumble at me, even with my face buried in a pillow at home. *Thanks anyway*, he'd said. *Thanks anyway.* He ambled off in his worn-out shoes.

I screamed into my bedding. I tried to rationalize it. Twenty dollars was two hours at the sub shop. It was a case of beer or some cheap oil paint. It's just, all these seemed increasingly pointless lying there, as the question of what those twenty dollars could've done for the singer burned right through the excuses I made.

For all I knew, he was huddled on a doorstep with his knees tucked under his chin. I imagined the man in such a state of despair that he would never sing again.

And to think it could've gone so differently. All I had to do was give him the money. If I had, he would've known that I recognized his pain. In that, we would've become friends.

He'd call me Music Guy when he introduced me to others. I'd call every label in town. I'd describe his voice as raw and urgent. He'd appoint me as manager of all his talents.

Together, we'd produce an album, maybe several, and there'd be tours, music festivals, platinum records hanging in the entrance of my home, which was not a basement, but a sterile white palace made of imported marble that overlooked the Pacific and its waves.

I ran for the door. I ran for the spot where I'd been stopped by the singer—where the Music Guy lived and died. I found him not a block down from where we'd met, outside the Hotel Le Marais.

The singer stood in front of a family of four who wore cotton hats with velcro at the back. He belted another Sinatra tune, and when he finished, the family clapped for him.

He shook his head. *It wasn't good*, he said.

Nonsense, the family said. The mother tried to push a small stack of bills into his hand. *Take this*, she said, but he turned.

He trudged in my direction with his eyes trained low. He would've walked right past if I hadn't stopped him.

Singer, I said. *I came back. I feel bad about earlier.*

I told you no pity, he said. He tried to push by, but I caught him by the shoulder and held on.

Then sing again, I said to him. *Make me feel. Sing again.* I pulled the twenty dollars from my pocket.

The singer's eyes hardly glanced at the money. It felt like none of this should've happened outside. I wished then I hadn't come on some ill-founded fantasy. It was so much easier to loathe into my pillow.

The singer produced some tune I'd never heard. The notes came out flat and unenthused. And while I wanted to enjoy his work, wanted to ignore the squeaks and mid-lyric apologies, I didn't feel that same labor as before. What I found were merely notes strung together on a street corner in the city. When he finished, the singer knew it too. I tried to hand him the money anyway, but he shook his head.

Not a chance, he said to me.

C'mon, I said, but he turned away. I ran after him and pushed the bills into his chest. *Take it*, I said. *You need it. How are you going to get home?*

If he was meant to clock me in the face, it was then he would've done it. Instead, he only stared at my hand on his threadbare shirt and the twenty dollars flat beneath it.

I'll sing, he said to me. *I'll always sing*. A thud beat through his bones. I felt it in my fingers, and I feel it now. The canvas in front of me is an endless winter.

ZOO FEELING

Looking dumb has its advantages, and tonight I proved that point. As the only American at a Belgian house party in Antwerp, I found myself isolated for a time to the whims of conversation offered up to me in English, to which I responded in my usual manner of little eye contact, frequent pauses, and punctuations of nascent laughter whistling from my nostrils.

If I'm telling you the truth, I don't perceive myself to be overtly dumb, not that many people do, but perhaps just a tad bit unmoored. If being and appearing are two distinct spheres, too often I find myself caught between them.

It didn't help my cause that I wore a maroon velvet vest with no undershirt to the party. This, along with my trusty pair of armadillo skin boots and black pleather pants, created an image best summarized by a guy who introduced himself only as Motherfucker. He said to me, *If someone tells me that you are a cheap stripper, I believe it.*

While I later rehashed the zippiest comebacks I should've said (*Oh yeah, well you look like a skid mark sandwich,* among them), to Motherfucker's comment I could only nod, as I did to most of the observations tossed my way by the Belgian partygoers. I had the sense that perhaps people were talking to me as a form of pity, a way to include me in what was otherwise an orgy of Flemish conversation, light house music, and beer drank from any vessel that could handle it.

What nobody knew, not even my friend Jackie who invited me, is that I understood Flemish and could speak it with a moderate level of comfort. This is one of the two advantages I enjoyed of my Ghent-born parents, who later transplanted to Colorado, the other being a child-like discontent for most places I find my feet.

This Flemish secret proved to be the key to my evening and the successes I ultimately enjoyed.

Now you might think I'm some sort of dingus for keeping such a secret, especially one that presumably could've liberated me from the corner of the apartment I occupied, nearest the cheese plate, where I had a broad view of the crowd.

I'll admit that while it wasn't forthright, I had no ill intentions either. I simply wished to see what I could learn from these people and maybe find a little entertainment in the process.

Take, for example, a pair of women so beautiful in their raw Japanese denim jackets and wide-cut pants that I felt almost certain in their responsibility for global warming. As they dripped honey from a café spoon onto small wedges of Chimay cheese, one said to the other in Flemish, *Who the hell is that guy in the vest? He looks like a cowboy fucked a vintage store.*

Motherfucker said he came with Jackie, the other said. *He's some American in town for a musical.*

Where this musical bit started, I do not know, though I must admit I quite enjoyed the thought of it and found myself wondering, as one of the women bet the other a joint that she wouldn't come talk to me, what role I might play in, say, "Death of a Salesman."

I quickly deduced that I was not quite cut out for overt stage performance and instead imagined myself as one of those people clad in black who scales the catwalk high above the audience and moves lighting to provide a dramatic effect. I was imagining such a case, one where I swiveled a gigantic spotlight onto Willy Loman as he realized, as all men eventually do, that he is an utter failure in a world where he dreamt so big and achieved so little, when a finger pecked at my chest.

You look, how you say, like an exotic dog. It was the woman who had accepted the bet. *Why you stand in the corner with no one but the cheese? Why you don't dance with Jackie? She has killer moves, you know.*

I smiled a great big nervousness back at her and felt my shoulders hunch toward my ears. Here was a woman who wore the beauty of just-washed linens, so crisp and layered and fragrant. And I, now a pretend light guy on the set of Death of a Salesman, felt rather doglike in her presence and wished then only to obey her.

She waited for my answer, which came in unintelligible stutters that amounted to a shrug. This appeared to be an inadequate response, and the woman communicated this by yanking my vest. She said, *Come on, dog boy. Let me show you how the Belgians party.*

This was Sofia. Her friend's name was Angela. And together, the three of us stepped out onto a cantilevered balcony to enjoy the spoils of Sofia's labor. We blew herb smoke into the grey night of Antwerp, as I fielded the women's questions:

What did I think of Belgium?

Did I listen to hardstyle?

In America, can you buy a gun in the grocery store?

The weed loosened me some, such that I spoke in complete sentences and with a certain candor uncommon to my mouth. I told Sofia and Angela that I thought Belgium was beautiful and dirty, the middle child between France and the Netherlands. I told them hardstyle was a vibe when out at the clubs, though acid jazz was really more of my scene. And as for the Americans and their grocery store guns, I told them I figured it existed somewhere.

Sofia turned to Angela after a while and said in Flemish, *This guy is, like, very weird.*

I know, Angela replied. *I can't tell if he has perspective or if he's just a wackjob.*

I'm afraid it's the latter, Sofia said. They both turned to me then and smiled, handing the last of the joint over.

We're going now, Sofia said in English. *Nice talk.*

Yes, nice talk, Angela echoed. I tipped the joint at the two of them and said we'd catch up later, though by the speed with which they opened the French doors and stepped back into the apartment, I could tell they hoped this wouldn't be the case.

I remained on the balcony for a while, joined intermittently by small groups in need of a cigarette, night breeze, or some combination of the two. These people would look me up and down before sharing their names, which quickly became so jumbled in my brain that I just as soon started assigning them letters of the alphabet.

I believe it was E and F, a stocky man with a long mane of curls and his presumed girlfriend, who had such a dizzying array of tattoos that one might compare her arms and legs to a Jackson Pollock painting, who said that someone, a man inside, was hitting The Griddy but with little form.

His skip and arm swing were completely out of sync, F said to E in Flemish, and she swung her arms back to show him just how chaotic such dancing appeared. E, for his part, shook his head. His long locks swayed in the evening.

Maybe he came with our cowboy friend, E proposed in jest, nodding not so inconspicuously in my direction. F turned and gave me a smile when she noticed me looking back at her. She put an arm on E's back and drew on her cigarette.

That's one dance-off I'd like to see, she said with an exhale. *Chrissakes.*

It was this, this imagined scenario in which I had come to a party only to be laughed at for my dancing that gave me a distinct zoo feeling. Here I was looking through the glass, thinking that in the ignorance around me, I could observe this party and the humanity it contained as if a child wandering through the primate exhibit. Never before had I thought that perhaps the gorillas and orangutans and baboons look back. Perhaps they talk about us, as we stand there and gawk and shovel fistfuls of french fries into our mouths. Perhaps they make judgments about us based on our clothing, while we senselessly tap on the glass.

I guess that made me something of a zoo keeper—split between the worlds of animal and audience. I walked that fine line, understanding Flemish without belonging to it. I had the thought that when we tap on the glass, we're really just asking for a sign. And as the zoo keeper, I had something of a sense for those. I knew exactly how to make the animals dance.

I found Jackie wedged between a cluster of bodies who seemed new and unintroduced to me. She had a beer bottle in her hand, which she pointed with while she spoke. I had the notion she was coming into her own.

When she saw me, she screamed, *Heyyyyyy*, and threw her arms around me. *Oh my gosh, you have to meet everyone*, she said in English. She ushered me formally into the cluster where I traded a few strangled handshakes. Jackie explained to the group that I only knew English, and I nodded as dumbly as I could.

In response, I got that same nod back, all of us instantly distanced by my alleged handicap. I felt in their collective stare a desire to ask questions and make conversation, though this urge was ultimately overcome by the fear of appearing dumb or not speaking with grammatical precision. And so, a hefty silence washed over all of us, as we clung to beer bottles and their sour brown contents as a balm for such discomfort.

I was starting to run a nice little high by then and cared more than anything else about keeping it. I took Jackie by the hand and attempted to spin her in a circle.

Go to the dance floor with me? I said. I knew the answer already. Jackie is many things to many people, but she is first and foremost a human of the spotlight.

By then, I had known Jackie for just over a month, and only so because I commented on one of her Instagram stories. She has this whole account dedicated to foreigners and other wayward souls who consume digital content as a means of disassociating from their current disposition. @Jackie_in_Belgium it's called.

I reached out to her when I arrived in Antwerp feeling lonely and rather sexually deprived. While my hand was ultimately made to satisfy the latter, Jackie replied to my comment, the one encouraging her to keep making videos on how not to appear like a parasitic tourist, which catalyzed a little chit-chat between us. I took the opportunity to share that I'd recently visited the only two spots awarded her esteemed five-star rating on the weekly French Fry Review, eventually summoning the stones, when it became obvious that one can only talk about french fries for so long, to tell her that I planned on being in Antwerp for while and that we should meet, if she cared to, for a beer. In reply, Jackie said she loved to meet her fans and that a proper introduction to the city called for drinks overlooking the Grote Markt.

I'll admit I was naturally hesitant about my decision to solicit company from a person I'd never met and whose only dimension I knew was one of an assumed persona, a cultural figurehead who spoke with more authority on the Belgian way of living than birth alone seemed to merit.

I, of course, got over myself and any parading of higher morals I might have feigned when I recognized that I was really no different. Sure, Jackie thought highly of herself and equated followers to fans, likes to adoration, though try as I might to belittle such pursuits, I found that when I really drilled down and asked myself not to lie, Jackie and I desired the same sort of results in life. We sought people to listen and not think we're insane. We sought people to reach out and tell us that we're special.

I met up with Jackie the next weekend, and found her, despite continued attempts to get me to talk about Pete Davidson and Kim Kardashian, to be lovely. She wore a shag of curly hair the color of wet mud that crowded her forehead and almost touched her shoulders. She dressed in smart European clothing, all black, with cuffs at the wrists and ankles. When she hugged me outside of the café and said what a pleasure it was to meet, I smelled lavender, red grapefruit, and cedar wood on her.

Our conversation was quite the opposite of the melted back-and-forth I'd come to expect of myself. Rather, it was a free and flowing discourse ranging from topics of Kant to beer pouring to yes, Pete Davidson and Kim Kardashian and our respective theories about how real that relationship ever was.

So why Antwerp? Jackie asked eventually. *It's lovely, of course, but also—odd to me.*

Why's that? I said.

You're American, she replied. *Americans go to Paris and stare at landmarks.*

I nodded. *I guess I'm not typical,* I said with a wink in hopes that I might weasel out of providing a more genuine response. But Jackie pried and asked why that was. I suppose it was her attention, which felt warm and true, that caused me to offer up something of a little more substance.

Why that something was a maxim of my existential dread is a pursuit best left to the therapists. I came to Antwerp because my Auntie Blanche lives here and offered to rent me one of the many apartments she manages at half-price. This, along with my understanding of the language, was more than enough ammunition to invest in a new me, which I catapulted into headlong. I said none of this to Jackie though.

Instead, I told her, *I don't know how to be myself.*

And what does that mean? she asked.

Why don't you tell me? Who is the American visiting Paris?

She gripped her chin in thought.

This set us down a path of deep exchange on the dangers of generalizing culture, when individuality must be taken into account. At varying stages of the conversation, Jackie referred to me as a piece of shit, a hipster, and a man of noble pursuit—all of which served to reinforce the dissociated state of my belonging.

It was this, I suspect, Jackie's approval of how un-American I seemed to be, so unsure of myself, that led her to invite me to the party. *You won't know anyone,* she said, *but I promise they'll adore you. Who knows, might even be a good chance to pick up some Flemish.*

What I picked up, more than anything else, was that as E and F had shamelessly predicted, my dancing was not up to snuff. While I anticipated a sort of syncopated bob, perhaps made flashy with pumped fists or a hip thrust into the open air, dancing to Jackie and the crew of partygoers around us was a rigorously orchestrated affair. There were a number of moves that all of them seemed to share in common though customized with a personal twist. One of these included what I will call the spaghetti arms, which you might assume is rather similar to an orgasm of the upper extremities but in actuality was something more elegant.

The general movement is to raise one's arms laterally, ideally in the song's build-up, going higher and higher until the beat drops at which point the arms assume an energetic bravado. It's at this junction where one's individual style comes into play. I was partial to Motherfucker's tactic, which included a rather saucy waving motion while akimbo middle fingers rose from either of his hands.

It was this last bit that got me in trouble—not so much that I was flipping the others off necessarily but that stealing the flip-off was not allowed. It was Motherfucker's move, which he kindly reminded me of when I tried to copy him the first time.

That one is mine, he said, playfully pushing me in the chest. *You find good move. Your own.*

Honor among this odd and increasingly drunk corps of Belgian twenty-somethings was not a joke. It was something real and stuck to, and this became painfully obvious to me after trying Motherfucker's move a second time, after which he yanked me by the ear to the edge of the room.

That one is mine, he said again, pressing his broad figure up against me. *Fucking American*, he said. *Fucking American*, by which point people started to realize something was forming.

Motherfucker turned to address the bodies packed into the living room, most of which had stopped their movement. He said in Flemish, *Who wants to help me teach this little bitch a lesson?* The bass cut to silence.

He's just trying to dance. Let him be, Jackie said.

But he's doing my move, Motherfucker said back. He pointed out various people. *Would you do my move?* he asked. *Would you? Tell me you would do my move in front of me,* he said to a rather impish-looking guy in a fishnet tank top. The guy shook his head furiously.

Exactly, Motherfucker said and turned back to me. In Flemish he growled, *You see, you stupid yankee, there are rules here. There is culture. Clearly, you don't get that.*

Something about this must've been funny in a Belgian way, as Motherfucker proceeded to laugh with his mouth hung open, goading the others looking on to join. In the deep vibrato of his diaphragm, I imagined a world in which I could shrink down to microscopic size. I would become a germ, and no one would know if I was with them or if I wasn't, and in that way, obscurity would allow me to navigate that in-between space without all the issues and self-loathing.

To be clinical about it, I felt fucking lost right then— more than ever before. I thought of my two loving parents who encouraged me to be myself, to always be myself. And while kind in theory, this advice felt like a cage—one I wasn't sure if I was meant to break into or out of.

Mostly because I have many selves already with an infinite number more on tap. One day, I believe I'm a sporty guy who eats kale caesar salads and grunts while power cleaning at the gym while the next I'm flying my ass to Belgium because I look around at my life in Denver and only see grovelers in pursuit of the almighty dollar. On the third day, I'm some mix of the two with a mild depression dolloped on top, which makes me think I will continue to create lies for myself, in the name of searching for my true self, and I'll believe in these lies until they begin to lose their luster when I look in the mirror and feel discouraged by how little progress I've made.

Motherfucker slapped my cheek. *Hello?* he said in English. *You are there, cowboy?*

My consciousness surfaced to find that I was not microscopic or a germ but a sweaty twenty-six-year-old bearing the questions of a haughty Belgian.

You are ready for your lesson? Motherfucker said.

My feet were halfway on a vintage rug, halfway on a tile floor. The room stared at me, and I scanned it to find that no one else would deliver me from this evil. I stood alone in my enclosure.

And in that particular loneliness, I expected to be crushed by the weight of my own passivity. But something strange bubbled up in my nuggets—a grounded feeling that positioned me squarely as the observed. They're tapping, I thought. Sofia and Angela and Jackie and all of them were tapping on the glass.

I stepped to Motherfucker, toe-to-toe.

Though he was a good six inches taller than me and had a goatee that made me question whether or not he'd once led an illegal strip-mining operation in Brazil, I made my eyes meet his. I said in Flemish, *Fuck off.* Then hearing myself speak, felt more confident, *Let's go, Motherfucker. You and me.*

Clearly, I was off my rocker, one moment cowering in the corner, the next standing with some spine. But it was more than this, wasn't it? It was that I'd revealed my Flemish secret—a secret that I'd hidden so well behind a façade of idiocy so easily attributed to my kind—which now caused the others in the room to reflect. What had they said to me, about me, likely right in front of my face? In their confused looks, I gained real power. The chimpanzees know when they're putting on a spectacle.

I unbuttoned my maroon vest and swung it over my head. *Make space, make space,* I said in Flemish. *We're doing this. We're duking it out.*

The bodies shuffled to the perimeter of the room, leaving Motherfucker and me in the center.

I put a finger in his chest and said, *You pick which side you want.* He slapped my hand away with no effort at all.

You sure you want this? he asked. *I'll mop the floor with your ass.* I looked up at the furies reticent in those dark eyes of his and knew he was probably right. Motherfucker was probably going to destroy me. He wasn't going to hold anything back. How often does one get the chance to set an American in his place? And at home? In the company of good friends?

I blew Motherfucker a kiss and said to him, *Your fly's undone.*

I pointed to Jackie, who stood ready with the aux and played the first track of battle on my signal. Motherfucker, looking up from a zipper that was as closed as it'd ever been, was already two moves behind me. *Dance off!* I screamed.

I have little doubt that I lacked technical proficiency, though I like to think I made up for it by doubling down on zeal. I fancied myself as demonstrating a juvenile grace found only in those pure moments where the heart leads and the body follows.

Jackie later described my dancing as the energy of a coke addict with the discomfort of a thigh rash. If I'm honest, I can't recall much of my display. In that moment, I was so close to the feeling that it became impossible to see much of anything. And the good news is that I didn't need my eyes. In all circumstances, they likely would've hurt me.

Apparently, Motherfucker was a classically trained danseur noble, and imposing as he might've looked, his grace on foot was something lighter than a bee landing on a tulip. He'd allegedly done a backflip and then dropped right into the splits. I saw none of it.

I merely blossomed with each song and let the speaker's vibrations rise through my legs. That gave me the energy to kick and to whirl and to shimmy while shouting great Flemish phrases into the air. *Maak dat de kat wijs! Nu komt de aap uit de mouw!* The crowd lapped me up like a dog.

I probably lost that dance battle by a mile, but by the time I stopped to look around and know it, I found a smile in the crowd made for me. I reached my hand out, and Jackie took it. I twirled her into my chest.

You're an idiot, she said.

Forever, I said and waved at the others to come and join us.

GOD WEARS A HARD HAT

There may come a rare moment in life—when all else can and has failed—that you find yourself like me: looking at a Dutch guide named Jan in the middle of Bali's Ubud Forest, saying, *This parrot is shagging my head*. And indeed it will be true, truer than the laugh Jan gives in reply, as he pulls a phone from his fanny pack to record a video. *Very good*, he says. *You are bird sexy.*

I do my best to smile, though when I see the footage later, it more so resembles a grimace. Who can really blame me? Sixteen pounds of ruby-colored bird, wings raised like a priest, thrust awkwardly into the back of my neck. The parrot's talons rip at the skin around my shoulders, so soft and pale and forgotten.

And it would be better to laugh, wouldn't it? That would make the whole of it digestible—the fact that I'd come to Bali in the first place amidst the hell storm of small-town politik back in Indiana. At the very least, laughing would remind my former wife, Christina, were she ever to see the footage, that although she seemed intent on sharing my every shortcoming as a husband and father to the world, I was getting along just fine with the parrots. Yes, laughing would be the appropriate retribution, all but making up for her latest comments, the ones to the Parent Teacher Organization, where my ex-wife described me as a fumbling turd in the sack, going so far as to say, *He ought to return to high school anatomy class. You'd think the clitoris was the Holy Grail the way he struggled.*

I do not laugh. I weep fat tears and continue to grimace, wondering why I bother. Why put up with a world that allows parrots to perch on one's shoulders and hump away to their content? Why live a life in which one's mistakes are ammunition? Am I ever allowed to be weak?

I cannot say. I run too much. I place most of my faith in silence. Maybe this is what got me here, falling to my knees, with a great red bird making love to the back of my head while a Dutchman tapes it. Maybe it's the silence that makes the breath hard to find. Maybe it's just this muggy jungle.

Or maybe it's none of this.

Maybe the world was built crooked from the start, a project mismanaged by god. And it's this thought, the one where god wears a hard hat and studies the blueprint to this world, scratching at a temple, that brings me a little peace. This god who struggles with calculus and feels insecure about the appropriate amount of cookies to eat after dinner. It can't be just one, but is three too much? God thinks, depends on the size.

I tear the parrot from its mount, and the bird seems surprised by my action. It squawks in a guttural sound of dismay, or maybe thrill, as I hold it in front of my face. The parrot's wings flap wildly against my grip, the feathers cooling from red to blue. And though it reaches for my fingers and tries to break them in its beak, when I use my dad voice, I take control.

No bite! I command. Everyone listens, and for a moment, I overcome the jungle.

Its orchestra of green falls silent before Jan says, *You can't kill this bird in the open.* The chirrups of insects, the howls of monkeys, the bird twitters—all of it returns.

I look at Jan, stringy hair pushed back. His face is stricken with fear. I try to see what he sees: a man so despairing, so trodden by Earth's beauties. A man ready to kill for trespasses.

But I am not this man. Jan hardly knows me. In fact, he knows me even less when I kiss the parrot between its big black eyes and set it free. Its ruby-colored body lifts into the treetops, a sun against those leaves. I stare at that sun before I feel it, rising from the pit of my stomach. It pours from my lips, a whinny of laughter, that spins out into the sky. I watch it rise above my head until it disappears, along with everything else.

Acknowledgements

Portions of this work were previously published in a different form in the following publications:

The Elko Butter Chase — *New Ohio Review*

God Wears a Hard Hat — *The Los Angeles Review*

Little Battles — *Raleigh Review*

Making a Music Guy — *Broken Tribe Review*

THE AUTHOR

J. Dominic Patacsil is a fiction writer based in Washington, D.C. He was awarded the 2023 Los Angeles Review Flash Fiction Prize, and his stories have appeared in *New Ohio Review, Third Coast Magazine,* and *Raleigh Review,* among others. He is a graduate of the MFA program at the University of New Hampshire. *Bald Spot* is his debut collection of stories.